Books
[All are available on Amazon and Kindle]

Ventryvian Legacy
[Science Fiction/Fantasy]

Wizard's Gambit
Kings and Vagabonds

Historical Fiction

Nicodemus' Quest
Saul's Quest
Joseph's Quest
The Making of the President:
The Nightmare Scenario

Humor/Fractured Fairy Tale

Ronald Raygun and the Sweeping Beauty

Drama/Plays

Sweeping Beauty [comedy]
Celestial Court [Christian]

Historical Fiction:

Nicodemus' Quest—The Jewish Supreme Court known as the Sanhedrin had already found Jesus Christ guilty of blasphemy and condemned him to die, setting in motion the events culminating in his death by crucifixion a few hours later. Why then would two of the most influential members of the Sanhedrin risk alienating their colleagues by removing Jesus' body from the cross and giving him a proper burial? Didn't they realize it was a lost cause—that Jesus' death proved he couldn't be either the Messiah or the son of God?

Yet Nicodemus and Joseph of Arimathea risked everything they had worked so hard for throughout their lives by identifying with Jesus at a time when even his friends and disciples had deserted him. What had they learned in their investigations into Jesus' background and ministry that caused them to take such drastic action? For that matter, why had they investigated him in the first place? Is Jesus the Messiah—and what relevance does that have for us two thousand years later?

Joseph's Quest— Are you facing problems, obstacles, or challenges in your life? Does it feel as if you've been broken beyond repair? Are you in need of a friend? Or a helping hand? Or a role model?

Meet Joseph. He was betrayed by his own jealous brothers, who dropped him into a pit while they considered whether to kill him. He was sold into slavery and later unjustly accused and wrongfully imprisoned. But his true story shows it is possible to overcome the problems, obstacles and challenges of life and eventually come out on top.

Science Fiction / Fantasy

Wizard's Gambit— Out of the thousands of planets searched by unmanned space probes, sixteen have both water and an atmosphere similar enough to Earth's to make colonization feasible. These planets have been listed as being Earth Virtual Equivalents—or EVEs.

A power struggle is developing on Eve Twelve that could have far-reaching consequences, the ripples from which could even reach and impact Earth.

Wizard's Gambit is the story of that conflict.

Kings and Vagabonds continues the story.

Fractured Fairy Tale:
Ronald Raygun and the Sweeping Beauty—COLE

BLACK RAYGUN might be a well respected king, but he still had a problem. Yes, it's true old King Cole had a reputation for being a merry old soul, but at the moment he was definitely not feeling particularly merry. Frustrated would be a more accurate word. Frustrated by that stubborn and obstinate son of his!

Although Crown Prince Ronald Raygun was heir apparent to the throne, it was not at all apparent who his bride— the future queen—would be. Ronald had never met a girl he liked enough to date more than a few times, much less to consider marrying. And old King Cole desperately wanted to spoil some grandchildren before he died. Luckily, King Cole can call upon the services of his Royal Attorney, Lord Shyster, who helps him find the necessary Royal Loopholes in the law that requires royalty to only marry other royalty or nobility . . .

Although this fractured fairy tale primarily satirizes the classic *Cinderella* tale, it also manages to fracture *Sleeping Beauty* and *The Princess and the Pea* . . . while also having fun with various politicians and other celebrities. But are you astute enough to catch all the hidden meanings and references?

All titles are available on Amazon.com and Kindle.

Saul's Quest

By the author of *Nicodemus' Quest*

Bill Kincaid

Although *Saul's Quest* is a work of fiction, many of the characters in these pages lived, and the scenes depicted have been reconstructed as accurately as possible from data available to the author at the time the book was written. Various modern English translations of the *Bible* have been used as a basis for the scenes and dialogue, though additional dialogue has been invented from the author's imagination in order to make the scenes flow more smoothly.

Copyright © 2019 by Bill Kincaid.

All rights reserved.

Published in the United States of America.

ISBN-13: 9781691318704

Dedicated to A. L. Teaff

Introduction

Few men have affected human history as much as Saul of Tarsus. He was born to devout Jewish parents who diligently followed and practiced traditional Jewish laws and customs, and Saul's early childhood and Hebrew education probably mirrored that of many other Jewish lads.

But Saul's intellect, reasoning, persuasive powers, and passion soon began to set him apart from his contemporaries. He was accepted as a student and disciple of Gamaliel, the Pharisee and Sanhedrin leader widely recognized as the foremost Jewish teacher in first century Judea.

Not only was Saul accepted as a Pharisee, but he even became a member of the Sanhedrin at a remarkably young age. He was well on his way to making his mark as a Jewish rabbi and theologian.

But then he was tapped by the Jewish high priest for a mission that was especially suited for a passionate person like Saul. He led the charge against the upstart followers of the Way, a group of people who claimed that Jesus of Nazareth was the Messiah prophesied by Jewish prophets of old. Even worse, many of them had the gall to claim Jesus was the Son of God! Saul agreed with the high priest that such a claim was obviously blasphemy and could not be tolerated.

Saul became the supreme human enemy of the early church, persecuting it and its believers and doing his best to wipe it out. Armed with letters from both the Jewish and the Roman authorities, Saul boldly pursued Jesus' followers wherever they ran, arresting them and carrying them back to the religious authorities in Jerusalem. He then would vote to convict them at their trials before the Sanhedrin.

Then came the day he journeyed to Damascus—and experienced one of the greatest life changing experiences in recorded history.

Walk with Saul on his momentous journey that radically changed not only his life, but also the history of the world.

Ananias

Ananias awakened from a troubled sleep. Nightmares generally fade quickly from memory as conscious thoughts replace the ethereal wisps of subconscious dreams—but this one was different. It had been especially vivid, and still burned in his memory like a festering sore.

In his dream, Ananias and a friend were being chased by a band of men. Ananias' friend tripped, fell, and was quickly surrounded by their pursuers. When he tried to get up, they knocked him back down, tied his hands, and took him prisoner. Then the ruffians continued chasing Ananias. No matter where he turned, Ananias' path was blocked by men who were either chasing him or who were dragging away other friends as prisoners.

Dreams are strange things. Sometimes you *know* something without being aware of precisely how or why you know it. In this case, Ananias somehow knew that the men chasing them had been sent by Jewish religious authorities and that capture meant almost certain torture or death.

For months, the high priest and his henchmen had been rounding up followers of Jesus of Nazareth and putting them into jail. Several of Ananias' friends had been beaten or flogged with whips, and at least one of them had been stoned to death.

In his nightmare, Ananias could barely run fast enough to elude his pursuers. He woke with a start when his wife shook him.

Ananias looked around frantically. His running legs had kicked the cover off his bed, and he was breathing hard and covered with sweat.

"What happened?" she asked worriedly.

"I dreamed the persecutors of the church in Jerusalem were coming after us to drag us back to the high priest and the council. It was awful."

"It was just a bad dream. Calm down."

"But it was so real. So vivid. I could even recognize our friends . . . and some of the ones who were persecuting us."

"Just relax and compose yourself. I'll get us something to eat."

"Very well, Rachel," he replied as he sat back and looked around him. With the exception of the displaced covers on his bed, all appeared to be normal. The chairs and table were still in their proper place, the gray and brown stones forming the walls of his room looked familiar and comforting, and no ruffians appeared to be lurking anywhere.

After composing himself for a few minutes, Ananias rose and walked to a wash basin. He poured some water from a pitcher into the basin and washed his face. He then slipped a *me'il* cloak over his undergarment and sat back down to consider the nightmare he had experienced.

Suddenly he felt as if he was surrounded by a bright light that obscured everything else.

"Ananias," called a voice out of the light.

"Yes, Lord?" he answered.

"There is something I want you to do."

"What is it, Lord?"

The bright light dissipated, and Ananias saw a man kneeling down before him, deeply engaged in prayer.

"I want you to go to the house of Judas on Straight Street."

"Is that the wealthy merchant named Judas?"

"Yes, that's the one. Ask for a man from Tarsus named Saul, for he is praying," the voice continued. "In a vision he has seen a man named Ananias come and place his hands on him to restore his sight."

The man kneeling in prayer in Ananias' vision raised his head and looked at Ananias. It was the leader of the ruffians who had disrupted his sleep in his nightmare!

"Lord!" exclaimed Ananias. "I have heard many reports about this man and all the harm he has done to your saints in Jerusalem. Now he has come here with authority from the chief priests to arrest all who call upon your name."

"Ananias, trust me. Go do what I tell you to do. This man is my chosen instrument to carry my name before the Gentiles and their kings and before the people of Israel."

"But, Lord. He'll kill me. Many of your followers have suffered immensely because of this man."

"I will show him how much he must suffer for my name—but I need you to trust in me and do what I have asked you to do."

"Yes, Lord," Ananias answered, and the vision faded from his sight.

Ananias took several deep breaths before standing and looking around the room. He realized he would be walking into a den of his enemies. Yet he was supposed to lay his hands on the most dangerous man he could think of and help restore that man's sight. His body was wracked with an involuntary shudder at the thought.

"Is something wrong?" Rachel's question shook him out of his stupor.

"I'm not sure."

"Why? What happened?"

"The Lord just gave me a task I'd rather not do." Another spasm shook his body.

"What's the assignment?"

"I am to go down to the other end of our street and help restore the sight of Saul of Tarsus."

"Saul of Tarsus?"

"Yes."

"Are you sure?"

"I'm afraid so."

"That's crazy. Isn't he the one who has been leading the persecution of the church in Jerusalem?"

"That's the one."

"That can't be right. You just got through dreaming about those awful men coming after us to drag us back to Jerusalem. Then you wake up and suddenly decide you are going to make it easy for them. You'll just walk into their house and give yourself up. Is that what you're saying?"

"Not exactly. God didn't ask me to give myself up. He just wants me to lay hands on Saul and help restore his sight."

"Oh, that's *really* an improvement! Saul can't persecute you effectively now because he has been blinded. But you are going to restore his sight so he can more easily arrest you? Are you out of your mind?"

"The Lord told me that Saul was his chosen instrument for spreading the gospel."

"He's really helped spread it, all right. Because of his persecution, believers have fled Jerusalem and have scattered across the Roman world. What will our friends think when they find out it was you who helped this awful man get back his sight so that he could continue persecuting the church?"

"I saw Saul in my vision. He was very earnestly praying."

"So what? After all, he is a Pharisee; they are always praying."

"No, you don't understand. He wasn't merely reciting a prayer; he was earnestly praying to the Lord. It was as if his world had been turned upside down, and he was asking God to reveal His will. The Lord said Saul had also received a vision. His vision was that I would be coming to him, laying my hands on him, and helping restore his sight."

Rachel suddenly broke down sobbing, "I don't want to lose you."

Ananias held her tightly in his arms and kissed her. "I love you, too."

"Don't go."

"I have to. We just have to trust the Lord in this."

"How do you know it was actually the Lord? Maybe it was just a continuation of your nightmare."

"No, this was different. I don't know how I'm sure it was the Lord. I just *know* it was."

"I still don't want you to go." She sighed and then added, "Please be careful."

"If you are worried about my safety, you can pray for me—and for Saul."

"I will. I love you. May God be with you."

"Thank you," Ananias smiled, and stepped out into the street.

Straight Street[1] was just that: a street that stretched out in a rather straight east-to-west line across Damascus. Ananias' house was near the eastern end of the street. In fact, from where he stood in front of his house, he could see the triple arches of the Roman Gate of the Sun, also known as the Eastern Gate. The large central arch was designed for horse-drawn vehicles, and was flanked by smaller arches for pedestrians.

Ananias breathed a quick prayer asking for the Lord's guidance and protection. Then he turned and headed west along a colonnade. An identical colonnade ran along the opposite side of the street. He passed various small shops, momentarily pausing as he realized that he might never see those familiar shops again. Nevertheless, since he had committed himself to being God's instrument, he pressed on.

About seven hundred meters west of the Eastern Gate, Straight Street intersected the Cardo Maximus, the primary north-south road in Damascus. Ananias walked under a large Roman arch that spanned the intersection, and then paused as he looked up and down both streets.

---

[1] Or Via Recta.

He and Rachel had lived all their lives in the city of Damascus. They were devout Jews who believed that Jesus was the Messiah promised by God and prophesized by various Jewish prophets over the preceding centuries. It was their custom to worship in the local Jewish synagogue each Sabbath, and to join their friends who also believed in Jesus the following day, which they called the Lord's day. That belief had caused them to be targeted for persecution.

Ananias continued west about another three hundred meters down Straight Street, pausing in front of the large house belonging to Judas, a well-known local merchant. This is where his vision had directed him to come.

Ananias hesitated before knocking. He looked down and thought wryly to himself, *My knees are already knocking.* He again said a prayer for protection—this one somewhat longer than those before it—and knocked on the door.

No answer.

Good, he thought, and was tempted to leave.

He knocked again. A servant girl opened the door.

"Is Saul of Tarsus here?" he asked.

"Yes, sir."

"It is imperative that I see him immediately."

The girl nodded her head and said, "Follow me."

She led Ananias to a nearby room. On a mat in the center of the room sat a man deeply engaged in prayer. The scene was just as it had appeared in Ananias' vision. He froze as he looked at the man on the mat, realizing that Saul had come to Damascus for the express purpose of arresting and carrying away Ananias, Rachel and their friends. *As long as he is blinded, he may not be as much of a threat. But the Lord wants me to help him.* Ananias felt as if his heart were in his throat, his breath was labored, and he felt faint.

At any moment Saul's band of ruffians could seize him and carry him away. Ananias gulped, took a deep breath, and walked toward the man who haunted his sleep—the focal point of his nightmares.

1.

I was in the dark. Literally, figuratively, physically, mentally—in every way possible, I was surrounded by darkness. Never before had I experienced such an utter and complete absence of light. Oh sure, my eyes were wide open—but I could see nothing, even though my senses were straining to do so.

But that wasn't the worst part of it. Far more troubling was the mental blindness and spiritual paralysis that gripped me like a vise. This was something totally new for me. For the first time in my life, I found myself unable to cope . . . and not sure what to do about it.

How did I come to be in this condition? It's quite a story, and as with any story, I should probably start at the beginning.

My name is Saul. I was born to devout Jewish parents who diligently followed and practiced traditional Jewish laws and customs. My father was a Pharisee, as was his father before him.

Although my early training and education was from my family and my local Hebrew school in Tarsus, my family sent me to Jerusalem as soon as it was practical for me to go. My father made arrangements for me to personally study at the feet of Gamaliel, the Pharisee and Sanhedrin leader who was widely recognized as the foremost teacher in all of Judea.

After visiting with me privately and probing my knowledge of the law of Moses, the history of our people, the writings of the prophets, the psalms, proverbs, and other wisdom literature, Gamaliel allowed me to become one of his students or disciples.

I spent each day with Gamaliel and his other disciples in the temple at Jerusalem, but the students slept in separate quarters from him at night. Most of our instruction and questioning occurred in one of the private rooms in the Royal Portico, a large colonnade that ran along the southern wall of the temple. Since the colonnade was completely covered by a magnificent roof, we could continue working there in all types of weather.

Gamaliel, however, would often lead us to various parts of the temple to make some points more memorable or to illustrate other points. For example, he led us into the Court of the Gentiles[2] to show us the lambs and doves available for penitents to purchase for sacrifice.

"Why are such animals permitted in a holy temple?" Gamaliel asked us.

"To be used as a sacrifice," answered a fellow student named Jonathan.

"What kind of lamb is required?"

"One without spot or blemish."

"Why?"

"Because that is what the law of Moses requires."

"Correct, Jonathan—but why would Moses write such a thing?"

"Because that is what God commanded."

"True—but why would God command that?"

Silence. Gamaliel looked intently at each of us. Finally, I timidly replied, "Such a lamb would be the best of the flock. God deserves our best. Also, it would be a financial sacrifice

---

[2] A huge open rectangular area about thirty-five acres in size bounded by the outside walls of the temple compound that was open to all people. Only Jews were permitted to go beyond the Court of the Gentiles into the Court of Women, and only Jewish men could proceed beyond that point.

as well as a literal sacrifice to part with the most nearly perfect lamb in your flock."

"Very good, Saul," Gamaliel smiled. "And why would someone willingly part with such a lamb?"

"So that their sins might be forgiven?"

"True—but tell me how killing a lamb causes forgiveness of one's sins."

"Because that's what God said he would do."

"Yes, that's true—but I want to know *why* God would make such a requirement."

This time the silence was deafening. We stood there mutely before our master. Finally he relaxed his stern look. "Think about what sin does," he prodded us gently.

"Oh!" I gasped. "Sin separates us from God. It breaks our fellowship. So God had to make a way for us to bridge the gap between our sinful character and his holiness. The way God chose to do it was by requiring us to bring a lamb without spot or blemish as our guilt offering."

"Yes! That is what I wanted you to see. God's sense of justice requires that one's sins be paid for with a blood sacrifice. It is the human who sinned and deserves to die for that sin. But God is willing to reconcile us to him by allowing us to substitute the blood of an innocent lamb for our own blood. This graphically shows God's mercy and forgiveness."

We watched as a lamb was sold to a man, who then led it back to his waiting wife and son. We followed them through the Court of the Gentiles and the Court of Women. All three members of the family walked up the fifteen steps leading from the Court of Women to the Nicanor Gate. Since only Jewish men are allowed to enter the Court of Israel, the wife stepped back and watched from the gate as her husband and son took the lamb to a priest, who slew the animal and offered it as a sacrifice on the large altar.

On another occasion, Gamaliel took us to one of the gates separating the Court of the Gentiles from the Court of Women. Pointing at the wall that separated Jews from

Gentiles, he asked, "Why do we make this distinction between Jew and Gentile?"

"Jews are God's chosen people," responded Joseph, another of the students.

"Explain what you mean," replied the teacher.

"God chose us as his special people."

"Yes, that's what you said the first time. I asked you to explain what you mean."

Joseph looked at the rest of us with eyes pleading for help.

"God promised Abraham that he would be the father of a great nation that would be God's special people who would be set apart to him," Jonathan said.

"Abraham was the father of many nations. What makes us special?"

"Jews are descendants through Isaac, Abraham's legitimate son through his wife, Sarah."

"Yes, but after Sarah died, Abraham married Ketuah and had six legitimate sons through his second wife. Their descendants are the Asshurites, Letushites and Midianites. The Arabs are descended from Ishmael, another of Abraham's sons. God also promised that Ishmael's descendants would be a great nation. In other words, I am looking for another distinction."

"God made a covenant with Abraham that Isaac's descendants would be the channel by which God would bless all the peoples on earth," said Jonathan. "We are God's special covenant nation."

"Very good," Gamaliel smiled. "And how has that covenant been modified?"

No one said anything for several moments. I shrugged and said, "God repeated and renewed the covenant with Isaac and Jacob. Later God modified it by promising David that from his lineage would come a great king who would rule his people forever."

"Has that great king yet appeared?"

"I don't think so. We are still being ruled by foreign Gentiles."

"What is the name or title given to this anticipated great king?

"The Messiah or the Christ."

"Why two names or titles for the same king?

"*Messiah* is the Hebrew title, while *Christos* is Greek."

"Which means?"

"The anointed one."

"Anointed with what?"

"Well, many kings and priests have been anointed with oil. The Messiah is to be anointed with the power or spirit of God himself."

"Very good. We Jews are God's covenant nation because of the covenant God has made with us over the years—especially the covenants with Abraham, Isaac, Jacob and David. I think there are at least two major reasons God chose us for this mission. You have mentioned the second reason, Saul: A Jew descended from King David will be the promised Messiah who will be a blessing to all the peoples of the world. What would be the first or more immediate benefit from having a covenant nation?"

After a minute of silence, Jonathan asked, "Maybe the law of Moses?"

"You're on the right track, Jonathan—and the law is a good portion of the answer."

"God intervened in human history to reveal himself to Abraham, Isaac, Jacob and their descendants so that we could better know the Creator," Jonathan said.

"Excellent. In a world whose peoples worshipped man-made gods depicting aspects or portions of God's creation, at least one nation would interact with the Creator himself. God explained what he wanted and how we could establish a relationship with him—and God gave us his law and his commandments. He also gave us his word, which has been preserved through the ages. We Jews are to be a beacon to the rest of the world so that they may also come to know God, his law, and his blessings. God told us how he wants us to approach him so that we can have a relationship with him."

As I sat in my prison of darkness, I thought about how my own relationship with God had progressed, and I wracked my brain trying to decipher precisely what had happened to cause me to be so misguided. *How could I have been so wrong?*

2.

Gamaliel stood in front of his students holding an artist's drawing. "What does this picture depict?" he asked.

"The Temple of Artemis in Ephesus," Jonathan answered.

"Good, and who is Artemis?"

"She's a fertility goddess in Greek mythology."

"Correct. Now, what about this picture?" asked Gamaliel as he held up a second drawing.

"That's either Zeus or Jupiter."

"How can you tell?"

"Bearded man throwing thunderbolts."

"Tell me about this picture," said Gamaliel as he held up another drawing.

"That looks like the Parthenon."

"And what is the Parthenon?

"Temple in Athens honoring their patron goddess Athena."

"And what about this drawing?" asked Gamaliel as he held up a fourth picture.

"I don't know, Master. A man whose head looks like a bird?"

"Maybe he's a bird brain," joked Joseph.

"His clothing appears to be Egyptian," I remarked. "And that fat snake over his head is mostly a sun-like disc. Is that the Egyptian deity Ra?"

"Right you are, Saul. Now, students, what do all these drawings have in common?"

"They all honor pagan gods?" Jonathan answered.

"Very good. How many pagan gods are there?"

Only our sighs and breathing disturbed the silence as we looked at each other and shook our heads. Finally Joseph said, "I don't know, Master—but it would be quite a few."

"Do each of the nations worship multiple deities?"

"We don't—but the others do," I said.

"How many gods do we worship?"

"Only the one true God."

"What is his name?"

"Yahweh."

"Which means?"

"I AM."

"What does it mean when God says 'I AM'?"

"That God actually exists; he is," I said.

"Yes . . . Continue . . ."

I fought a brief moment of panic as I attempted to think of what else I could say. After a few seconds, I added, "We humans can debate all we wish about whether there is a god or precisely how many gods there may be. But no matter what we decide among ourselves, our conclusions do not bind God or change the fact that he does exist; He *is*."

"Very good, Saul. What else does 'Yahweh' mean?"

Silence. Gamaliel looked intently at each of us, but none of us said anything.

"What tense is the verb?"

"Present tense, Master," said Joseph.

"That should give you a clue."

We just looked at our teacher with blank expressions. After a minute of silence, Gamaliel sighed and said, "Let me give you another clue. What is the difference between God's relationship to man and man's relationship with all the pagan gods?"

I timidly ventured, "God created man, who in turn created the pagan gods?"

"Yes, Saul; God is the Creator, while both man and his pagan gods are part of the creation. Now, how does that relate to the 'I AM' that God calls himself?"

We just sat there. Minutes ticked by before Gamaliel eventually nodded, smiled, and gently explained, "When we talk about an object being three-dimensional, we mean that it has height, width and depth. You can measure our precise location by setting forth our longitude, latitude and altitude. I am standing at a measurable point where those three planes intersect. Do you understand what I am saying so far?"

We all nodded, and Gamaliel continued.

"In other words, we are limited by the dimensions of the universe in which we live. I cannot be at more than one place at the same time. However, the Creator of the universe is not limited by the dimensions of his creation. God can be anywhere and everywhere at the same time. This is what we mean by being *omnipresent*. Have I lost any of you yet?"

We shook our heads *no*.

"The fourth dimension of our universe is time. We can only move forward in time, one second at a time."

Gamaliel searched our faces, and we nodded that we understood.

"Once again, the Creator is not limited by the dimensions of his creation. Therefore, God is not limited by the dimension of time any more than he is limited by the other dimensions. Thus, God *is* yesterday, he *is* today, and he *is* forever. When God says 'I AM,' God is also expressing the truth that he is forever in the present tense."

"Oh!" I gasped. "Are you saying that God is simultaneously at all points in time?"

"That is precisely what I am saying. That is why God knows the future and can reveal information to his prophets."

I felt as if a window of knowledge had been opened, and I had caught my first glimpse through it.

"There is at least one other meaning for 'I AM' which you should know," Gamaliel continued.

"The phrase God used at the burning bush with Moses can mean either 'I AM who I AM' or 'I AM who I choose to be.' God is a spirit or spiritual force who can appear to us in any manner he chooses to do so. What are some ways he has appeared to men?"

"He spoke to Moses out of that burning bush," Jonathan said.

"Pillar of cloud and a pillar of fire," Joseph added.

"He walked in the Garden of Eden," I said. "And he spoke to Elijah out of a whirlwind."

"His glory filled both the tabernacle and Solomon's Temple when they were first dedicated," added Jonathan.

"We are told that Jacob wrestled with an angel," I said. "But since God changed Jacob's name to Israel—meaning one who wrestles or contends with God, perhaps God appeared as an angel. And the spirit of God also hovered over the waters of creation."

"Yes, but remember that the Hebrew word for waters can also mean a chaotic mixture," Gamaliel cautioned. "Moses might have been telling us that God's spirit directed the creative process to bring order out of chaos."

We sat still for a few minutes as we contemplated the various aspects of God's holy name. Then Gamaliel turned to me and said, "Saul, you said earlier that we worship only the one true God. How do you know there is only one God and that he is the true one?"

I thought for a moment before answering. Then I said cautiously, "Only one God has revealed himself to mankind, and he said he is the one and only Supreme Being who created all else that is."

"Good response, Saul. I had anticipated I would need to probe with additional questions, but I think I can use your response as a teaching point."

Gamaliel looked intently at each of us and then asked, "Have any of you personally met Yahweh?"

We shook our heads.

"Have any of you personally met any of the pagan gods?"

We again shook our heads.

"Then how do you positively *know* which is the true God—or even how many deities there may be?"

"That is what we have been taught, Master," replied Joseph.

"Yes, that is what you have been taught. But what you learn is generally only as good as it is truthful, reliable, and trustworthy. How can you be certain that what you are taught meets those criteria?"

We looked at our teacher and at each other, but no one spoke.

"Anyone?" Gamaliel prodded after a few moments, searching each of our faces.

"Well," I eventually stammered. "I guess the first test might be to examine our sources."

"What do you mean?" Gamaliel asked.

"If our source for certain information has established a history of being truthful, reliable and trustworthy, it is more likely that the new or untested data will also be reliable."

"Excellent. This was the principal test for God's prophets of old. Since many people claimed to be God's prophets, their words were written down and then compared with the events that actually occurred. Only those whose prophesies were truthful, accurate and trustworthy were deemed to actually be true prophets of God. So tell me, Saul: How confident are you that what you have been taught about God is accurate and trustworthy?"

"Everywhere I look, I see evidence of a world designed by a Supreme Intelligence; I don't think that just happened by chance. When I pray about a problem, I receive answers I had not previously considered; I suspect that's not an accident. When I read scripture, I obtain insights that are more relevant and personal than those I find in other religions or philosophies; that implies a divine intelligence inspiring the writers of those scriptures. The histories set forth in scripture are accurate, and the prophesies have been fulfilled. I am confident that what we have been taught about God is true."

"Very well. Tell me about God."

"There is one—and only one—God who created everything else that exists. God is the Eternal One who lives forever and can never die. He made a covenant with Abraham that although Abraham would be the father of many nations, one of those nations would be God's special people with whom he would make a covenant. That covenant said that God would raise up a great king from the descendants of King David who would rule his people forever and through whom all the nations of the world would be blessed."

It had all seemed so clear and simple to me then. I felt certain that everything was just as I had said; it was true, reliable and trustworthy. But now I knew I had to make an adjustment in what I thought and believed to accommodate what I had recently learned.

3.

My memories refocused on an event several years later. Like my father and grandfather, I was admitted into the very select group of Jewish religious leaders known as the Pharisees. Although I was no longer a student of Gamaliel, our relationship had grown into a friendship.

There were times we would have a meal together, and Gamaliel sometimes invited me to accompany him on short journeys, most commonly in or around Jerusalem. We occasionally journeyed to the Essenes community at Qumran, which was located in some caves in a dry plateau about a mile inland from the northwestern shore of the Dead Sea. Although Qumran is only a few miles from Jerusalem, the area is rugged and Gamaliel did not like to make the trip alone.

One such trip we had intended to take was interrupted by a sudden change in plans.

"I'm sorry, Saul," Gamaliel said when we met, "but the high priest has asked members of the Sanhedrin to go down to the Jordan River to check out a new holy man who is apparently causing quite a stir."

"What's he doing?" I asked.

"As far as I know, he's calling for people to repent of their sins and be baptized. But the high priest is concerned that he might be another self-proclaimed Messiah who could start another rebellion."

"Why is that his concern?"

"Well, Saul," Gamaliel chuckled, "you have to understand Caiaphas' point of view and all that he stands to lose if the Romans have to crack down on a rebellious people. The Romans have largely allowed us to have a free rein with regard to our faith and the practice of our religion. The temple priests and Sadducees live rather comfortable lives that could be torn apart if the Romans cracked down on us."

"Very true. Roman legions are not particularly known for their mercy and gentleness when they punish a rebellious people."

"That could be the understatement of the year, Saul. Anyway, Caiaphas has asked as many members of the Sanhedrin as are able to do so to check out this apparition from the wilderness. Would you like to accompany me?"

"I would be most honored."

"Thank you, Saul. We can go to Qumran another day."

We headed east from Jerusalem along the Jericho road. After passing the Mount of Olives and a few small villages, the road began winding down the steep incline into the Jordan River Valley, which extends from the Sea of Galilee in the north to the Dead Sea in the south and is entirely below sea level.[3]

The people split into roughly three groups as they reached the bottom of the valley. The largest number continued along the road into Jericho, while the smallest group continued eastward toward the Jordan River to a place where they could cross over to the east bank. We joined a sizeable number of folks heading north along the west bank of the Jordan until we found the holy man we were seeking, who was known as John the Baptist.

John was a wild-looking young man with long coal-black scraggly hair and beard, and he wore a garment of camel's hair. He had a leather girdle about his waist, and stood in a small pool about twenty feet from the western edge of the Jordan River. The pool was one of several that formed when

---

[3] The shoreline of the Dead Sea is the lowest point on the Earth's surface not covered with water. The Jordan River Valley is part of the Great Rift that extends approximately 3,700 miles—or 6,000 kilometers—from northern Syria to an area surrounding Lake Victoria in southeastern Africa.

the waters of the river slowed prior to pouring into the Dead Sea.

Two men stood to the left of John as he faced the crowd on the river bank. The water came up slightly above their waists.

John took hold of one of the men and announced with a loud gravelly voice, "I baptize you with water, but one is coming who is mightier than I, the strap of whose sandals I am not worthy to unfasten." John lowered the man beneath the water before speaking further. As he raised the man back up, John continued, "He will baptize you not with water, but rather with God's Holy Spirit . . . and with fire."

As John moved to the other man, he bellowed, "His winnowing fork is in his hand, and he will thoroughly clean his threshing floor." He lowered the second man under the water and began to raise him back up before saying, "He will gather the wheat into his barn." John gazed over the crowd as he continued, "but the chaff he will burn with unquenchable fire."

John's eyes rested on part of the Sanhedrin delegation. "You brood of snakes!" he exploded at them. "Who warned you to flee from the wrath to come? Show by your actions that you are really and truly repenting. God expects more than mere religious dogma and pretended piety."

"How dare you speak to us like that!" one of the Sanhedrin—a Sadducee named Matthias—responded indignantly.

"Do not think that you will be saved merely because you are a descendant of Abraham!" warned John. "Do not excuse your actions by telling yourselves that 'We have Abraham as our father.' I tell you most earnestly that God is able to turn these stones into children of Abraham. The wicked kings of Israel were also children of Abraham, but that did not save them. You must truly repent of your sins and accept God's mercy and gift of righteousness if you are to escape the coming judgment."

"Who are you to warn me about judgment?" asked Matthias. "I am a Sadducee and a member of the Great Sanhedrin."

"Do you produce good fruit for the Lord?" John replied. "Even now the axe is laid to the root of the trees. Every tree which does not bring forth good fruit will be cut down and thrown into the fire. Make certain, therefore, that the fruit you bear is good and pleasing to God, and that it brings glory to God Almighty."

"Then what should we do?" shouted someone in the crowd.

"If you have two coats, give one of them to someone who has none. If you have excess food, share it with others who need it. If you are truly a child of God, you should help and share with your brothers and sisters."

The man at the front of the line on shore called out to John, "Master, I wish to be baptized—but I am a tax collector. What should I do?"

The Jews near the man quickly moved away from him, since they despised Jews who made large profits off their countrymen by collecting taxes for the hated Roman government.

"Do you truly repent of your sins?" John asked.

"I do."

"Have you sacrificed a lamb at the temple for your sins?"

"I have."

"Do you vow that you will never again collect more taxes than the amount appointed you by law?"

"I promise and bind myself accordingly."

"Then come forward and be baptized," John commanded.

"And what about us?" two Roman soldiers on the river bank yelled out. "What should we do?"

"Do not extort money from people by violence or bring false charges against anyone," John responded. He then added as an afterthought, "And be satisfied with your wages."

The two soldiers mumbled to each other as they moved toward the back of the crowd.

After several hours, someone finally asked John if he might possibly be the Messiah.

"Although I am the son of a priest, I am merely a man," John replied. "I'm not the Anointed One, but am only the voice of one crying in the wilderness to prepare the way for the Lord. The one coming after me is mightier than I am. In fact, I'm not worthy to touch even the hem of his garment. He will make straight the paths of the Lord, and will save his people from their sins. He is the Lamb of God who takes away the sins of the world, and who will be a blessing for the peoples of all nations."

As we walked back toward Jerusalem, I asked my old teacher what he thought of John the Baptist.

"I didn't particularly like his insinuation that I was part of a brood of snakes," Gamaliel replied. "Nevertheless, I found his discourse to be rather interesting—possibly even enlightening. It's obvious he's familiar with the writings of the prophets Isaiah and Malachi."

"What do you mean?" I asked.

"Those prophets said that before the Messiah comes, there will be a messenger who will prepare the way, crying in the wilderness, 'Prepare the way for the Lord; make his paths straight.'"[4]

"That's almost exactly the words John used to describe himself!" I remarked.

"Yes. That's why I said it's obvious he is familiar with the writings of those prophets."

"Is John claiming to be the messenger who is to prepare the way for the Messiah?"

"I got that impression."

---

[4] Malachi 3:1; Isaiah 40:3.

"Do you think he could be the messenger and that the Messiah might be about to appear?"

"I suppose that's possible, Saul—but I try not to get too caught up in looking for the Messiah."

"Why not?"

"Quite frankly, there are too many scriptures that could be prophesies about the Messiah, and they don't always appear to be consistent with each other."

"What do you mean?"

"Well, we generally think of the Messiah as being the great king who will sit on his ancestor David's throne and rule his people forever. Right?"

"Yes."

"The most detailed messianic prophesy we have comes from Isaiah, who spoke of how the Messiah's kingdom would never end. But Isaiah also wrote about the Messiah being a suffering servant who would be beaten and bruised for our sins.[5] The two pictures don't seem to jibe. Also, Daniel says the Messiah will be cut off or killed.[6] Cut off from what? Killed? How does that fit in with a king who will rule his people forever?"

"Is that why we didn't study the Messianic prophesies as thoroughly as we did some other scriptures?"

Gamaliel gave me a hard glance. Then he flashed a sheepish grin, nodded, and said, "You caught me, Saul. I concentrated on how the Messiah would be a fulfillment of God's covenant with Abraham, Isaac, Jacob and David, but skipped some of the prophesies that seem to be at odds with each other."

"Do you know anything else about John?"

"Not really. Well, other than what he had to say about himself." Gamaliel's voice trailed off and he mused to himself a few moments before continuing, "Come to think

---

[5] Isaiah 52:13-53:12.
[6] Daniel 9:26.

of it, I am almost positive I may have seen him previously. In fact, I believe I've seen him several times."

"Where?"

"In the Essenes community at Qumran over the past couple of years."

4.

Within a few months, rumors began spreading about a new rabbi named Jesus who had been identified by John the Baptist as the mighty person of whom he spoke. It was said that he had the power to miraculously heal people. As a result, large crowds followed him wherever he went. It was reported by several sources that the crowds in Capernaum were so large that friends of a paralyzed man found it necessary to make a hole in the roof of a building where Jesus was teaching and let the paralyzed man down through the hole in order to get him to Jesus to be healed.

Although the new rabbi was generally popular with the people, he also created controversy by taking liberties with law, scriptures, and tradition. For example, before he healed the paralyzed man in Capernaum, Jesus first told the man, "Your sins are forgiven." Since God is the only one who can forgive a person's sins, Jesus probably committed blasphemy by claiming to forgive the man's sins. Similarly, it was reported to us that he healed people on the Sabbath—even though the Law of Moses forbids working on the Sabbath.

My first opportunity to see the man in action came when he showed up one day at the temple in Jerusalem. As soon as I heard he had come, I hurried to where I could quietly observe him and see what all the commotion was about.

He put on a show, all right—but not the kind I had expected. Instead of working any miracles, Jesus assaulted some people in the Court of the Gentiles, the temple's large outer courtyard that is open to everyone—male and female,

Jew and Gentile. People of all races gather in this massive thirty-five acre enclosure to listen to various rabbis teach, to visit with other folks, or to transact business. Since Roman coins were considered unclean or defiled, such monetary units were typically exchanged for temple coins at the tables of the official money changers. The temple officials set the exchange rates, which guaranteed a tidy profit for the temple.

The market where live animals could be purchased for sacrifice was also located in the Court of the Gentiles. Technically, the penitent who was offering the sacrifice was supposed to bring the best lamb he had from his own flock. However, many of them either came farther than would be convenient for bringing the lamb or were not herdsmen and would have had to purchase the sacrificial animal somewhere. Making animals available in the temple was both simpler and more convenient for the penitent, and it was more profitable for the priests who rented out the space used by the sellers of the animals.

I saw Jesus watching both the money changers and the sellers of sacrificial animals. He saw several families be turned back by priests because the animals they had brought with them did not meet the priests' standards. The dejected people had no choice but to purchase livestock offered by the temple sellers, who took the rejected animals as trades and gave partial credit toward the purchase price. I knew that the "rejects" were generally sold a few weeks later as prime sacrificial animals.

Jesus did not appear to be amused by such "good business" tactics. He walked over to an area where some loose cords were lying on the ground, picked up the cords and made them into a makeshift whip. He then turned on the livestock sellers with a vengeance, brandished the whip as a weapon, and overturned their tables.

"Take these things out of here!" he ordered. "Do not make my Father's house a market place!" Jesus also turned over the tables of the money changers.

Attracted by the commotion, Caiaphas hurried to where Jesus continued his assault on the tables. "Just what do you think you are doing?" the priest demanded.

Jesus replied, "It is written, 'my house shall be called a house of prayer'—but you have turned it into a den of thieves."

"I am the high priest of this temple," Caiaphas responded haughtily, "and I have authorized these people to offer their services as a convenience to the people. What sign can you show us for your authority to overturn these tables and cause such a disruption?"

"Destroy this temple," Jesus said, "and in three days I will raise it up."

"You are a madman!" interjected Matthias, who stood beside Caiaphas. "This temple has taken forty-six years to build—and it's still being worked on. Yet you claim you will rebuild it in only three days!"

I noted with wonder that Jesus' presence was so commanding that he appeared to have a greater aura of authority than did the Jewish officials who opposed him. Neither Caiaphas nor Matthias could maintain eye contact with Jesus. Rather, Matthias soon hung his head toward the ground, while Caiaphas moved over to join a group of Jewish leaders. Money changers frantically picked up spilled coins, while livestock sellers rounded up their loose animals.

Jesus, on the other hand, turned to the crowd of people that had been attracted by the commotion and began teaching them as he sat down in an area at the top of the steps near the portico where Jewish rabbis often discussed points of Mosaic Law.

"Do not allow yourselves to be so attracted to riches or monetary gain that you lose sight of the more important treasures God has in mind for you," he said.

"Similarly, do not store up treasures for yourselves here on earth, where moths and rust destroy and where thieves break in and steal. Rather, store up treasures in heaven for you and your family. Remember that where your treasure is, there will your heart be also."

* * * * *

I continued to watch and listen to Jesus over the next couple of years, and I listened to my fellow Pharisees as they discussed his actions and teachings. Although I was impressed by Jesus' speaking ability and compassion and was awed by his almost supernatural ability to heal people with serious ailments and infirmities, I was greatly concerned by his rather casual attitude toward a couple of God's commandments.

The fourth of the Ten Commandments given to Moses was to keep the Sabbath holy and to avoid working on that day: "Remember the Sabbath day by keeping it holy. Six days you shall labor and do all your work, but the seventh day is a Sabbath to the Lord your God. On it you shall not do any work." Yet Jesus repeatedly healed people on the Sabbath, and he allowed his disciples to pluck grain from stalks as they were passing through wheat fields on the Sabbath—a clear violation, since harvesting grain is considered work.

I once confronted him about the problem by pointing out, "God commanded us to observe the Sabbath day and keep it holy. Yet you have violated the Sabbath by working on that day. You have healed lepers, given sight to the blind, and made the lame walk—all on the Sabbath. How do you justify your actions?"

"Let me ask you a question," Jesus responded. "Moses commanded that a boy be circumcised on the eighth day after birth. If that day is the Sabbath, you still will circumcise him on that day so that the Law of Moses might not be broken. Why then are you angry with me because I made a man's entire body well on the Sabbath?"

It was an excellent question. I didn't know what to say. When I made no reply, Jesus continued, "Do not judge merely according to your prejudices or appearances, but rather be honest and fair in your judgments."

Although I could not fault Jesus' statements or logic, it upset me that he had embarrassed me in front of crowds of people. I resolved to do better in our next encounter.

*****

"What is the purpose of the Law of Moses?" I asked Gamaliel one day as we were sharing a meal.

"What is the purpose of any law?" he countered.

I thought a moment before answering. "I suppose laws provide a framework or set of rules."

"Why is that needed?"

"To prevent chaos and anarchy, to promote harmonious living in a society, and to provide an orderly means for settling disputes?" I responded uncertainly.

Gamaliel nodded his head slightly, and then asked, "How do laws do all those things?"

"The state prohibits certain conduct by making it a crime. Other laws establish rules or guidelines for interpersonal relationships in a society. For example, laws govern property ownership, marriage and divorce, other family rights, contractual matters, and means for resolving disputes."

"Very good, Saul. So what would be the purpose for the laws God gave to Moses?"

"Hey!" I objected. "That's what I asked you to start with!"

"So you did," Gamaliel chuckled. "I suppose it is difficult to move away from my teaching mode after all these years. However, now that you are not only a Pharisee but have also joined me as a member of the Sanhedrin, you are now my peer instead of merely being my disciple. Fair enough; you asked me first . . ." His voice trailed off before continuing.

"The Law of Moses does include rules for society as a whole, such as the ones you mentioned. But the Torah also includes laws regulating the priesthood, sacrifices and offerings, feasts, and even ceremonial rules pertaining to purity and what might cause a person to be ceremonially unclean."

Gamaliel smiled as he added, "Moses spends more time and verbiage discussing the garments to be worn by the high priest than he does on God's creation of the heavens and the Earth and all that is in them."

"Interesting point," I said, "but what do you think is the principal purpose?"

Gamaliel thought a moment, nodded, and answered, "Because Moses received much of the law from God, it is largely concerned with what God wants and expects from us, how to establish a relationship with God, and how to reconcile and rebuild our relationship when we sin."

"How does the law do all that?"

"God gave us commandments he expects us to obey. If we fail to do so, we commit a sin that breaks our fellowship with God. However, since God wants to maintain a relationship with us, his law also outlines procedures for us to follow that will reestablish our relationship with him."

I thanked Gamaliel and built on the framework he had outlined for me to construct an argument that would enable me to overcome Jesus' arguments when I next met him. Unfortunately, I never got the chance to use it.

5.

I received an urgent message from home that my father was gravely ill and hoped to see me before he died. Naturally, I changed my plans, immediately wound up my affairs in Jerusalem, gathered my few possessions, and left for Tarsus.

Tarsus was one of the greatest cities in the Roman Empire, ranking alongside Athens and Alexandria in population, wealth, culture and commerce. It was the capital and most important city of Cilicia, and was located on the coastal plain about ninety stadia[7] from the northeastern edge of the Mediterranean Sea. Although there were strong heathen influences present in the city, a sizeable community of Jews also lived there, and we had several local synagogues. My father was a Pharisee and a rabbi in one of the synagogues.

As soon as I got to town, I rushed to him. He appeared to be hanging onto life by a precarious thread.

"*Abba!* Papa!"

He opened his eyes and broke into a broad smile, attempted to lift his right arm, and sputtered, "Saul! It's good to see you."

"It's good to see you, too, Papa."

"Listen to me, son. I don't know if I'll have strength to tell you all I want to say, so listen carefully."

"Yes, Papa."

"When I am gone, you will be the man of the house . . ."

"No, Papa, you're not going to . . ."

---

[7] Approximately ten miles.

"Saul! Please! I asked you to listen and not interrupt."

I nodded as he gripped my hands in his and looked earnestly into my eyes.

"When I am gone, you will be the man of the house. Look after your mother as best you can. My old trusted servant Ezra has been taking care of my affairs the past several years. He knows all about our property and can help you manage everything."

I nodded again.

"Please take my place at the synagogue at least until other arrangements can be made. You are also a Pharisee, have been trained by Gamaliel himself, and now are even on the Sanhedrin itself."

He held my hands in his, looked intently into my eyes, smiled and said, "I'm so very proud of you."

I blushed and looked down nervously.

He patted my hands and added, "You'll do fine."

I just looked at him.

"Will you do that for me?"

"Yes, Papa."

"You promise?"

"If it's that important to you."

"It is."

"Then I promise."

He died six days later. I worked with Ezra and my mother to settle his estate and resolve the loose ends. I also met with others in the Jewish community in Tarsus, and was warmly received by them.

Weeks stretched into months, but the days seemed to fly by as I was lost in my work. Although some in our local synagogue were initially hesitant to embrace me as rabbi, my enthusiasm, dedication, and knowledge of the scriptures seemed to win them over.

I was able to use many of the arguments I had prepared for using against Jesus in my teaching at the synagogue. Several of the younger men were especially enthusiastic followers. They, in turn, brought in other young men from the Cilician region around Tarsus, and I began training them almost as disciples.

One day a Jew named Jacob brought news of what had happened in Jerusalem after I left for Tarsus.

"Do you remember that teacher called Jesus who upset many of our religious leaders by healing people on the Sabbath?" Jacob asked.

"Yes," I answered.

"He really caused a stir shortly after you left."

"What did he do?"

"He raised a man named Lazarus from the dead . . . four full days after he had been buried."

"Is that even possible?"

"Apparently. Three members of the Sanhedrin confirmed that they had personally interviewed the people who had washed and prepared Lazarus' body for burial. Two of them had also been present for the funeral and had watched Lazarus be buried."

"But I thought the soul only hovered around the body for two or three days; four days would be too long a time for someone to be brought back to life again."

"As your old teacher Gamaliel pointed out, that old theory is apparently not correct. Anyway, large numbers of people decided Jesus must be the promised Messiah. On the Sunday before Passover, crowds laid their coats and palm leaves before him and Jesus rode into Jerusalem on a donkey almost like a conquering hero—but less than a week later, he was dead."

"Dead?"

"Yes. Crucified by the Romans."

"I guess that proves he's not the Messiah."

"I would think so," Jacob said. "That should be the end of that movement."

Such was not the case, however, as I learned a couple of weeks later from a Jewish merchant named Titus.

"Jesus' followers are claiming he rose from the dead and has appeared in person to them," Titus said.

"Surely not," I responded. "Did someone steal his body from the grave?"

"That's what our religious leaders are saying."

"Weren't any precautions taken to keep that from happening?" I asked.

"That's the wild part. Both temple guards and Roman soldiers were posted around the tomb to keep Jesus' body from being stolen."

"And it happened anyway?"

"Apparently. Our leaders claim the body was taken while the soldiers were asleep."

"What happened to the soldiers who let it happen?"

"Nothing."

"Nothing? Isn't that odd?"

"Extremely. Usually a soldier who is caught sleeping while on guard duty is severely reprimanded . . . or killed—especially if the person he is guarding escapes. Odd, don't you think?"

"Very much so," I said. Little did I know just how unusual it was about to become—or how much it would affect my own life.

6.

We Jews celebrate Passover to commemorate the freeing of the children of Israel from bondage in Egypt. God Almighty in effect declared war on Egypt's gods by inflicting ten plagues on Egypt. The Egyptian gods were powerless to prevent any of the plagues. The tenth and worst of them was when the Lord's death angel killed Egypt's first-born children and cattle. The Israelites were instructed to spread the blood of lambs across the doorposts of their homes. The death angel passed over the homes that were thus marked.

Fifty days after Passover we observe *Shavuot*,[8] which commemorates God{'s} giving his law to Moses and the Israelites at Mount Sinai. Although I normally would have journeyed to Jerusalem for the festivals associated with *Shavuot*, this year I stayed in Tarsus in order to finish some tasks I had started. Therefore, the first indication that something unusual had happened in Jerusalem came when a local synagogue regular named David returned to Tarsus with a rather strange tale.

"I'd never seen or experienced anything like it," David said excitedly.

"What are you talking about?" I asked.

"I was walking along one of the southern streets in the upper, newer part of Jerusalem when I heard what sounded like a mighty rushing wind. I looked up but saw no storm clouds. The wind seemed to pass right over me. I followed

---

[8] Also known as the Festival of Weeks, the Feast of Firstfruits, and the Festival of Reaping. Because it is fifty days after Passover, it is also called Pentecost.

the sound and watched as the 'wind' struck a nearby house. Instead of being blown apart, the upper room of the house appeared to be filled with intense brilliant light. Almost immediately, men began rushing out of the house and into the street. Hundreds of other people came running from all directions, apparently also attracted by the noise and strange light."

I looked at David with a confused expression.

"The men who came out of that upper room had faces that glowed with an unnatural radiance—almost as if their faces had absorbed some of the brilliant light that had filled the room. What was especially unusual about it is that I could clearly understand every word those men were saying—understand them in my own native Cilician dialect. Although they claimed they were speaking Aramaic, others understood them in each person's own native language."

"What do you mean?"

"Romans understood them as if they were speaking Latin, Greeks as if they were speaking Greek, Egyptians as if they were speaking Egyptian, and so forth."

"That's impossible!"

"I know! That's what makes it so incredible."

My dubious look only seemed to spur David on.

"I asked one of the glowing men what was happening," David continued.

"What did he say?"

"He said they had been filled with the Spirit of the living God."

"What's that supposed to mean?"

"I don't know. The man next to me laughed and said that it was more likely they had been filled with spirits of strong drink."

"Was there any response to that accusation?"

"Yes. One of the glowing men—a fellow called Peter—denied that they had been drinking and pointed out that it was both too early in the day for that sort of thing and that liquor doesn't cause people's faces to radiate light. Peter claimed this was a fulfillment of some prophesy the prophet Joel had written."

"What prophesy?"

"I don't remember, but Peter quoted it just fine—or at least it sounded good to me. Anyway, he went on to assert that someone named Jesus had worked many miracles and mighty works throughout the land. Many in the crowd affirmed that the statement was true. Peter than claimed that Jesus had died at the hands of wicked men who crucified him. God, however, raised Jesus from the dead."

"What was the crowd's reaction when Peter said that?"

"A few were offended, but most were listening very intently. I was still hearing him in my native dialect, which made it much easier to comprehend everything."

"Please go on with your account. Sorry I interrupted."

"Peter referred to several Messianic prophesies he said Jesus had fulfilled, and asserted that this showed Jesus was the promised Messiah."

"I thought the Messiah was supposed to live and reign forevermore. How can he do that if he died?" I asked.

"If he was raised from the dead, what would keep him from reigning?"

"The last I checked, we were still under Roman occupation. Where is this so-called Messiah's throne?"

"Peter claimed Jesus had ascended into heaven."

"Oh, that's convenient."

"Just be aware that about three thousand people agreed with what Peter said, accepted Jesus as their Lord and savior, and then were baptized into their fellowship just that one day—and I have heard there are more being added every day."

"So their movement is growing stronger instead of weaker?"

"So it seems."

How much it was growing became clearer to me a few months later when Jonathan, a friend and fellow disciple of Gamaliel, came to Tarsus to plead with me to return to Jerusalem.

"We need you and your leadership skills to help combat this new cult that is springing up," he exclaimed.

"Why? Has it grown that much since *Shavuot*?"

"Yes, and our leaders seem unable or unwilling to do anything about it."

"I had heard three thousand people joined their cause at *Shavuot*."

"That's true, though they refer to it using the Greek term *Pentecost*."

"What has happened since then?"

"Two of Jesus' disciples—Peter and John—healed a beggar who had been crippled from birth and who spent each day begging in the temple."

"Healed him? How?"

"The beggar had called out to them for alms. Peter responded, 'I don't have any money, but I will give you what I have. In the name of Jesus Christ of Nazareth, stand up and walk.' Peter reached out, gripped hold of the beggar's right hand, and helped him stand up."

"Was he able to stand?"

"Not only stand, but he was soon leaping and jumping around. He even picked up the mat he had been lying on—and danced around with it."

"And you saw all of this with your own eyes?"

"I did."

"Who was the man who pretended to be crippled?"

"I don't know his name, but he's been begging in the temple as long as I can remember. Do you remember the fellow who was always carried by his friends to the right side of the temple's Beautiful Gate?"

I thought for a few moments, and slowly remembered an elderly crippled man who was always there in the temple while Jonathan and I were being taught by Gamaliel.

"Yes, I think I remember him; at least forty-five or fifty years old, and said to be crippled from birth," I replied.

"That's the man they healed."

"Impossible!" I muttered. "Jesus might have been able to do it, but Peter and John were both just fishermen. I remember them well."

"Nevertheless, it happened just as I told you—and there were over a thousand people watching."

"Did our leaders do anything about it?"

"Peter and John were arrested and taken to the Sanhedrin, who questioned them and warned them not to continue speaking or teaching in the name of Jesus."

"How much good did that do?"

"None. They continued teaching and performing miracles."

"Right there in the temple?"

"Yes. Enough people came to the temple just to see and be healed by Jesus' disciples that the high priest ordered the temple guards to arrest all of Jesus' disciples."

"So they got all of them?"

"For a few hours, anyway. Somehow the disciples got free from the temple jail and went right back to teaching and healing in the temple courtyard."

"You're kidding. How did they escape from the temple jail?"

"No one knows. The next morning the high priest commanded that Jesus' disciples be brought to the Sanhedrin. Their cells were still locked and guards were posted outside—but no disciples were inside. It was almost funny watching the temple guards trying to explain how *that* happened. Then the guards found out the disciples were teaching outside in a temple courtyard—so they were rounded up and taken to the Sanhedrin."

"What happened?

"I've been told that the only thing that saved the disciples from severe punishment or even death was intervention by our old teacher."

"Gamaliel?"

"Yes, Gamaliel."

"What did he do?" I asked.

"Gamaliel reportedly reminded the council of several prior instances where self-proclaimed Messiahs had attracted a following. In each case, the movements fell apart when the leader was killed. He advised the Sanhedrin to leave Jesus' disciples alone. He said if their purpose is of human origin, it will fail—but if it is from God, we will not be able to stop them . . . and will only find ourselves fighting against God. The Council agreed and let the disciples go with only a flogging."

I was speechless for a moment. Then I shook my head and sadly said, "I'm sincerely disappointed in my old teacher and friend. He of all people should realize that crucifixion disqualifies Jesus of any possibility of being the Messiah."

"What do you mean?" asked Jonathan.

"Being crucified is basically the same as being hung from a tree."

"So?"

"The Law of Moses says that anyone who is hung on a tree is under the curse of God.[9] I believe that a man who is under the curse of God cannot possibly be God's promised Messiah."

"Makes sense to me," said Jonathan. "But each day dozens—maybe even hundreds—of people are joining the fledgling movement. That's why I've come, Saul. We need your help."

"What do you mean?" I asked.

---

[9] Deuteronomy 21:22-23.

"It's obvious that the older members of the Sanhedrin are afraid of the potential backlash if they kill or even severely discipline the core group of Jesus' disciples. Too many people flock to them for healing and blessing. But we must do something. Many of the younger Pharisees and Sadducees are frustrated and want to take action. We think you are the logical person to lead us."

"Me? Why?"

"Let's face it, Saul. The best educated young Jews in Jerusalem are those who studied at the feet of Gamaliel. We are the cream of the crop—and you are the most passionate, knowledgeable and charismatic of us all. You are a natural leader. That's why I was sent here to fetch you. We need you. Will you help us?"

I didn't know what to say. My mind swirled with jumbled thoughts. Finally I looked up into Jonathan's eyes and said, "Tomorrow's the Sabbath. Let me think and pray about it, and then join me at our local synagogue. After we finish with our worship time, I normally meet with some other young men who have become like disciples to me. Tell them what you have told me, and then we'll talk about what should be done."

7.

"What do you think I should do?" I asked my Cilician friends the next day after Jonathan had finished telling them about the growing Jesus cult. He concluded his remarks by again pleading for me to accompany him back to Jerusalem.

"I guess I'm being selfish," a Hellenistic Jew named Nicholas answered, "but I personally hate to see you go. I have learned so much from your teaching these past few months here in our synagogue."

"I agree," said another young Jew named Aaron. "But I also agree with Jonathan that you would probably be the most effective person to lead the assault against this false religion."

Several others nodded their consent.

"What do you want to do, Saul?" asked Aaron.

I thought a moment before answering. I finally shook my head and said, "I'm not sure. I have thoroughly enjoyed being able to explore the scriptures these past few months with my new Cilician friends here in Tarsus, but I also feel as if I may need to go back to Jerusalem. For one thing, I had just been made a member of the Sanhedrin shortly before I came back to Tarsus. I haven't really discharged my duties there the way I should . . ."

My voice trailed off and I failed to finish my statement. I looked into the eyes of the young men who had grown to mean so much to me as I had endeavored to teach them some of what Gamaliel had taught me. I saw in their expressions that they felt as I did . . . and understood.

"I seriously prayed about this last night," I continued, "and think the Lord may be leading me to go back to Jerusalem."

"Would you allow some of us to go with you?" asked Nicholas.

At first I was startled by the question, but then I nodded my head and replied, "I would love to have you there with me." I intently examined their faces as I continued, "Any of you who can do so are most welcome."

Thus it was that seven of them joined Jonathan and me when we journeyed back to Jerusalem. Since we traveled by ship from Tarsus to Joppa, I had ample opportunity to instruct my friends on major points where I thought the arguments espoused by the followers of Jesus might be especially weak.

"These 'believers'—as they sometimes call themselves—refer to themselves as being people of The Way."

"What Way?" asked Aaron.

"Jesus reportedly referred to himself as being 'the way, the truth and the life,' and claimed that no one can come to the Father except through him."

"The Father?"

"Yes. Jesus apparently referred to himself as being the Son of God."

"That's blasphemy!" Aaron exclaimed, but then he added less emphatically, "Isn't it?"

"Well, blasphemy is making oneself equal to God or claiming to be a god. Saying that God is his father would at least imply that he is equal to God or is a part of the Godhead. That's one of their arguments we need to counter."

"Agreed."

"They also claim Jesus is the Messiah. There are dozens—possibly hundreds—of prophesies about God's promised Messiah. While we are in Jerusalem, we should probably look at the scrolls of prophesy at either the temple or at Qumran. Make a list of the prophesies so we can refute that claim. That should be easy to do, since the Anointed One is supposed to live and reign forever. Jesus died, and he certainly hasn't replaced the Romans."

"What about their claims that Jesus was resurrected by God?"

"We need to earnestly examine anyone who claims to have seen Jesus after he was crucified. See what proof they can give. Check their stories for inconsistencies. I'm also curious about why the soldiers who were guarding the tomb allowed Jesus' body to be removed—and why those soldiers weren't punished. We need to get answers."

"Tell them about his being cursed of God," Jonathan prompted.

"Oh, yeah. That's another thing. Moses said that anyone who is hung on a tree is under God's curse. How can God's Messiah also be under God's curse?"

The others laughingly agreed.

"But remember one thing," I cautioned. "In order for us to legally put anyone to death, the Sanhedrin must find the criminal guilty of threatening to destroy the temple. Otherwise, even a person given a death sentence must be turned over to the Romans and tried under Roman law."

"How likely is that to happen?" asked Nicholas.

"Didn't Jesus say something about destroying the temple?" queried Aaron.

"Yes, but he didn't say he would do it," Jonathan replied. "When Jesus was asked about what authority he had, he responded 'Destroy this temple and I'll raise it again in three days.' He also said the time was coming when the temple would be destroyed along with the rest of Jerusalem."

*****

When we got back to Jerusalem, I found a couple of the soldiers who had guarded Jesus' tomb.

"What happened to Jesus' body?" I asked.

"His disciples came while we were sleeping and took it," one guard replied.

"While you were sleeping? Were all of you asleep at the same time?"

The soldier shrugged but said nothing else. I looked at his companion, but he avoided eye contact.

"How could you have allowed that to happen?"

No response.

"Were you punished?"

The soldiers looked at each other. One motioned with his head and then they both got up and walked away from me without answering.

"Wait. Aren't you going to answer?"

The second soldier turned and growled, "Talk to the high priest. We have nothing else to say about it." Then he turned and walked off.

Two days later I had the opportunity to talk privately with Caiaphas, the high priest. I told him about my conversation with the soldiers and asked him what had happened.

"Like the soldiers told you," he replied, "we think Jesus' disciples stole his body while the soldiers were sleeping."

"Soldiers who sleep while on guard duty are usually punished severely," I responded. "Were these soldiers disciplined?"

Caiaphas' face reddened, and he looked extremely uncomfortable. He glanced around to make certain we were alone. Then he leaned close to me and whispered, "Put yourself in our position, Saul. Jesus' body was missing, and we didn't know what had happened to it. The soldiers who were guarding the tomb came back with a wild story about an angel in brilliant radiant garments effortlessly rolling back the stone and allowing Jesus to walk free. We couldn't allow them to tell such a story at a trial—so we let them go without being punished."

I just stood there dumbfounded. Finally I simply asked, "What can be done about this new movement?"

"We have arrested Jesus' disciples; we've beaten them, flogged them, ordered them to cease and desist from preaching and healing in Jesus' name, and reminded them what we did to Jesus. If we killed their leader, we can certainly do the same to them."

"What effect has that had?"

"When we flogged them, they rejoiced that they were counted as being worthy to suffer for their Lord. When we ordered them to quit preaching, teaching and healing, they replied that they must obey God rather than men. In other words, nothing seems to work."

"What would happen if you killed one or more of their leaders?"

"We don't know. That's something we have been discussing. Your old teacher, Gamaliel, cautioned against doing anything like that. He said if this new movement is of men, it will soon disband, disperse, and come to nothing. On the other hand, if it is of God, we ourselves would end up fighting against God. Another problem is that Jesus' disciples are so popular with the people that we could start a riot by targeting them."

"What if you left the disciples alone but went after the new converts?"

"That might be a solution. If people who were less well known were persecuted and punished, others might be less willing to join the cult."

I thought about what the high priest said and compared it to what Gamaliel had told the Sanhedrin. *Which was the better solution?*

I watched and listened as Jesus' disciples preached, taught and healed people in and around the temple. Vast crowds flocked to them, and I witnessed many healings allegedly taking place.

What they had to say was revolutionary. No longer was Jesus presented merely as a good teacher or rabbi. Instead, they elevated him to a place equal to God himself. For example, John proclaimed, "In the beginning was the Word, and the Word was with God . . . and the Word was God. And the Word became flesh and made his dwelling among us. We have seen his glory—the glory of the one and only God. He came from the Father, full of grace and truth, and spread his light among us that we could see his truth and testify of his great redeeming power."

My mind reeled as John exclaimed, "Moses gave us the law, but Jesus Christ has given us grace and truth, which completes and surpasses the Law of Moses."

The words swirled in my brain. I had been taught to revere the Law, to place Moses on the highest pedestal imaginable, and to hold fast to the central teaching of Judaism: The Lord our God is the one and only supreme sovereign eternal Creator of everything. John, however, was claiming that Jesus was with God in the beginning, that together they had created the universe, and that his grace and truth were greater even than the Law of Moses.

It was such a radical message that I didn't even know where to start in trying to rebut it. Moses was the great lawgiver, wasn't he? Israel was God's special nation—the people of God's covenant. In a world of various peoples who worshiped man-made gods representing various aspects of creation, Jews were the people who worshiped the God who created everything else. These were the God-ordained channels of religious instruction I had been taught from the very beginning of Hebrew school. *How could John even dare to claim that Jesus was superior to Moses and equal to God himself? How could his grace and truth be above the Law of Moses?*

As I met with my Cilician friends, we resolved that we would dedicate ourselves to stamping out this dangerous new religion. Moses the great lawgiver would *not* be supplanted by a simple Galilean carpenter if we could help it!

8.

"The ancient Messianic prophecies have been fulfilled by Jesus of Nazareth," a Hellenistic Jew named Stephen proclaimed in the temple the next day.

"Then why are we still under Roman Rule?" Aaron yelled back at him.

"God sent Jesus into the world to save us from our sins, not to save us from Rome."

"I thought the Messiah was to sit on David's throne and would live and reign forever."

"Messiah is of the royal line of David and he does live forevermore—but his kingdom is a spiritual kingdom rather than a political one."

"That's not the way I remember the Messianic prophecies."

"Isaiah said the Messiah would be pierced for our transgressions, crushed for our iniquities, and oppressed and afflicted for our sins. He would be a guilt offering—the perfect sacrifice for our sins so that we can be redeemed and have everlasting fellowship with God. Jesus ushered in the new and better covenant that had been promised by Jeremiah."

Aaron fell silent and looked to Nicholas and me for help.

"Jesus was born of David's family, died as foretold by the scriptures in order to deliver us from Satan's power, and was buried in a rich man's grave as was also foretold by the prophets. On the third day he rose again as had been prophesied and is now exalted at God's right hand as Son of God and Lord of all."

"That's blasphemy!" yelled Nicholas, and he left to report his accusations to the high priest. Nicholas and Aaron were joined by other Jews from Cyrene, Alexandria, and the provinces of Cilicia and Asia, who collectively referred to themselves as the Synagogue of the Freedmen.

Caiaphas had Stephen arrested, and a trial was quickly arranged to be heard before the Sanhedrin. Although that ruling council was composed of seventy-one members who were appointed for life, the court could conduct business as long as it had a quorum of at least twenty-three members. The court sat in a semicircle with two clerks before them to record testimony and votes. Caiaphas and Stephen stood at the center of the semicircle in front of the assembled council. Since I was now a member of the Sanhedrin, I was able to sit in on all its proceedings and to attend Stephen's trial.

"I personally heard Stephen claim that Jesus is the Son of God and that he currently sits at the right hand of God," Nicholas testified. "In other words, Stephen asserts that there is more than one God."

A Jew from Alexandria pointed at Stephen and proclaimed, "This fellow never stops speaking against this holy temple and against the Law of Moses. In fact, I have heard him say that Jesus of Nazareth will destroy this place and will change the customs Moses handed down to us."

After several other witnesses gave similar testimony, the high priest turned to Stephen and asked him, "Are these charges true?"

I turned my attention to Stephen, and was surprised to see that his face seemed to radiate light. I quickly glanced from him to Caiaphas and other nearby men. It was no illusion. Stephen's face appeared to glow, but I could not think of any rational explanation.

Stephen looked over the assembled members of the court and implored, "Brothers and fathers, listen to me! The God of glory appeared to our father Abraham while he was still in Mesopotamia and said, 'Leave your country and your people and go to the land I will show you.'"

Stephen stretched out his left hand as if he were tracing a route on a map. "So Abraham left the land of the Chaldeans and settled in Haran. After the death of his father, he was sent by God to this land where you are now living. Abraham was given no inheritance here—not even a foot of ground—but God promised him that he and his descendants would eventually possess this land, even though at the time Abraham had no child.

"God told Abraham, 'Your descendants will be strangers in a country not their own, and they will be enslaved and mistreated four hundred years. But I will punish the nation they serve as slaves, and afterward they will come out of that country and will worship me in this place.' Then God gave Abraham the covenant of circumcision, and Abraham became the father of Isaac, who later became the father of Jacob, who in turn became the father of the twelve patriarchs."

Stephen's eyes swept over the Sanhedrin. His voice was mesmerizing as he continued, "Because the patriarchs were jealous of Joseph, they sold him as a slave into Egypt. But God was with him and rescued him by giving him sufficient wisdom and insight to enable him to gain the goodwill of Pharaoh, who made him second only to the king of Egypt in power.

"Then a famine struck all Egypt and Canaan, bringing great suffering. Joseph's wisdom allowed him to prepare for the famine so that Egypt had sufficient grain stored to survive. Joseph's father and brothers moved to Egypt with their families. Later another king, who knew nothing of Joseph, became ruler of Egypt. He dealt treacherously with our people and oppressed our forefathers by forcing them into slavery and killing their newborn babies.

"At that time Moses was born, and he was no ordinary child. He was rescued from Pharaoh's decree by Pharaoh's own daughter, who took him and brought him up as her own son. He was educated in all the wisdom of the Egyptians and was powerful in speech and action.

"When Moses was forty years old, he rescued a fellow Israelite by killing an Egyptian who was mistreating him. The next day Moses came upon two more Israelites who were fighting. He tried to reconcile them by saying, 'Men, you are brothers; why do you want to hurt each other?' But the man who was mistreating the other pushed Moses aside and said, 'Who made you ruler and judge over us? Do you want to kill me as you killed the Egyptian yesterday?' When Moses heard this, he fled to Midian, where he settled as a foreigner and had two sons.

"While Moses was tending sheep in the desert near Mount Sinai, he saw a bush that was burning but was not consumed by the fire. When he went closer to see why the bush was not destroyed, the Lord spoke to him, 'I AM the God of your fathers, the God of Abraham, Isaac and Jacob. I have seen the oppression of my people in Egypt and have come down to set them free. Now come, for I am sending you back to Egypt.'

"This is the same Moses whom they had rejected with the words, 'Who made you ruler and judge?' He was sent to be their ruler, judge and deliverer by God himself! Moses led them out of Egypt and did wonders and miraculous signs in Egypt, at the Red Sea, and for forty years in the desert."

Stephen paused momentarily before continuing, "This is the same Moses who told the Israelites, 'God will send you a prophet like me from your own people.' He was in the assembly in the desert, with the angel who spoke to him on Mount Sinai, and with our fathers; and he received living words to pass on to us.

"But our fathers refused to obey him. Instead, they rejected him and had Aaron make them an idol in the form of a golden calf, which they worshipped."

Stephen sadly shook his head, sighed and said, "Our forefathers had the tabernacle of the Testimony with them in the desert. Our fathers under Joshua brought it with them when they took the land from the nations God drove out before them. It remained there until the time of David, who asked that he might provide a dwelling place for God. But it was Solomon who built the temple for him."

Many of the members of the Sanhedrin were nodding in agreement with Stephen's words. His words intensified a bit as he proclaimed, "However, the Most High does not live in houses made by men. As the prophet says, 'Heaven is my throne, and the earth is my footstool. What kind of house will you build for me? Or where will my resting place be? Has not my hand made all these things?'"

Stephen gestured with both hands as he called out, "You stiff-necked people, with uncircumcised hearts and ears! You are just like your fathers: You always reject the Holy Spirit!" The council members stopped nodding their heads as shock replaced agreement.

"Was there ever a prophet your fathers did not persecute? They even killed those who predicted the coming of the Righteous One. And now you who have received the Law that was put into effect through angels have not obeyed it. Rather, you have betrayed and murdered the Messiah."

"This is an outrage!" howled a Sanhedrin leader named Matthias. I heard several similar but less articulated outbursts from other members.

Stephen, however, merely looked up toward the ceiling, pointed upward, and exclaimed, "Look! I see heaven open and the Son of Man standing at the right hand of God."

The witnesses who had testified against Stephen made loud cries of anguish and rushed toward him. Instead of attempting to stop them, Caiaphas merely stepped aside and allowed the young men to grab Stephen and haul him outside. I joined the other members of the Sanhedrin by following.

Stephen was dragged outside the city walls and thrown down into the nearby Kidron Valley. The young men who had testified against him laid their outer garments at my feet, picked up stones and began throwing them at Stephen. They were joined in the execution by several members of the Sanhedrin, although most of the court merely watched.

The strange glow on Stephen's face was finally obscured by blood and bruising. Above the curses of the executioners I heard Stephen's voice as he cried, "Lord Jesus, receive my spirit." Then he fell on his knees beneath the onslaught of stones. The last thing I heard him say was, "Lord, do not hold this sin against them." Then he died.

9.

"Saul, why did you allow the Sanhedrin to conduct such an illegal trial?" Gamaliel asked. My old teacher was obviously displeased.

"Allow?" I responded. "I'm a new member of the Sanhedrin. There are several on the council who think I'm too young to even be allowed to sit in on the proceedings. You're the Sanhedrin's president and are one of its most revered and respected members. Perhaps *you* should have done something if you think the trial was improper."

"If I had known about the so-called trial, I most certainly would have objected to not following our own Jewish legal requirements. For that matter, if it had been held over for a second trial on the next day—as is required by our law for capital cases—I could have made it back into town in time to take part."

"But Stephen committed blatant blasphemy in the presence of the entire council."

"I don't care if he did! Well, that's not true. I really do care, but that's still no excuse for not conducting a proper trial. As you should remember from our lessons, our law does not allow a capital case to be tried in one session. Rather, it must carry over to a second day in order to accomplish our rules of justice. If the court votes for a conviction, the Sanhedrin must adjourn without passing sentence. Only after it has reconvened the next day and the evidence is again reviewed may another vote be taken and sentence be passed."

"Well, at least the court did adjourn without passing sentence…"

"*Humph!* It's my understanding that the Sanhedrin didn't even take a vote before abandoning the *Liscat Haggazith*[10] to stone the man to death."

"You might note that the first stones were cast by the witnesses who had testified against Stephen."

"At least that small aspect of our procedural law was followed," Gamaliel grumbled.

*****

"I get the impression that our old teacher did not approve of the manner in which Stephen was tried," I later commented to Jonathan, and told him of our conversation. We were walking south along a road to the west of the Pool of Bethesda. Ahead of us on our right loomed the imposing walls of the Fortress of Antonia.

"I'm sorry Gamaliel feels that way," Jonathan responded. "Personally, I was almost ecstatic about how well the trial went. I thought we struck an important first blow against that cult."

"I agree—though I must admit that I was getting worried that Stephen might talk his way out of being convicted by the Sanhedrin."

"Very true. Did you see the way they were nodding their heads in agreement with what Stephen said?"

"Yes. I thought he had effectively rebutted the more serious charges against him. If he hadn't gone crazy at the end . . ."

"He would have probably gone free. Thank God he said those things about Jesus!"

"What caused him to do that, anyway?" I wondered out loud.

"Who cares? Just be thankful he did."

---

[10] The hall of polished stone where the Sanhedrin conducted its trials and deliberations

"No, really, Jonathan. Think about it. Stephen gave a brilliant condensed history of our people, including a synopsis of the roles played by Moses, the law, the tabernacle, and the temple. Had he continued speaking along those lines or even concluded at that point, he might have been released by the Sanhedrin."

"But he didn't."

"No, he didn't. Instead, he launched into an attack on the Sanhedrin. He reminded them that they had convicted Jesus, and said they were just like their stiff-necked and rebellious forefathers who killed God's prophets."

"Even then, he might have been released with just a flogging," said Jonathan.

I nodded my head in silent agreement as two Roman soldiers walked past us toward the Antonia. "What condemned Stephen was that he committed blatant blasphemy by declaring that he saw Jesus standing at the right hand of God in heaven."

"Agreed," said Jonathan, nodding his head.

"Why would he do such a thing?" I asked again. "Why would someone as articulate and intelligent as Stephen deliberately say things he had to know would incite the council?"

Jonathan merely shook his head helplessly.

"I tell you: These people are dangerously deluded!"

"What can we do?" asked Jonathan.

"Let's go to Caiaphas and offer our services. Let the high priest of God decide how best we can serve him," I answered. We continued our walk south toward the temple.

*****

Caiaphas listened to me and looked over the young men who were with me. Then he thought for a moment, smiled and said, "Yes, Saul. I think we can use your services. But I must warn you that there are certain risks involved. You will be despised, hated and feared by these people. Persecuting them might even involve breaking a few laws. *We* won't prosecute you, of course—and I can provide letters authorizing your actions, which should also help protect you."

"What about the Romans?" I asked.

"I can visit with Pilate, the Roman governor. If he refuses to cooperate, we can go over his head to Vitellus."

"Vitellus? Who's he?" I asked.

"He's the imperial legate. We have a good relationship with him, since he seems especially anxious to win our favor."

The high priest thought a moment, smiled, and continued, "Or we could go directly to Emperor Tiberius himself—and Pilate knows it. He is in no position to oppose us in this matter."

"Why not?"

"Pilate was a friend and political appointee of Sejanus," Caiaphas smiled. "And Sejanus was recently executed by Tiberius after the Emperor found out that Sejanus was responsible for murdering Tiberius' son. Let's just say that Pilate's position at the moment is precarious at best. I'll visit with him; he'll cooperate."

*****

"Caiaphas talked with both the Romans and with his friends and advisors within the Sanhedrin," I explained to the young men who had joined me in our project. "As long as we stay within their guidelines, we have been given a rather free hand to persecute these people who think Jesus is the Messiah."

"What are the guidelines?" asked Jonathan.

"We have to leave Jesus' disciples alone . . . at least for now."

"Leave them alone? Why?"

"They are apparently too popular with the people. The authorities are afraid that persecuting them might cause a riot."

"What are we allowed to do?"

"We can arrest any of the other followers of Jesus. We can't kill them, torture them or flog them—but we can arrest them and drag them from their houses, the synagogues, or other places where they meet or worship, and take them to the authorities to be jailed, tried, convicted, and punished."

We went over the lists of names and places that had been provided by the high priest. Many of the people belonging to the Way—as they called themselves—worshiped with other Jews in the temple or the synagogues on the Sabbath. Then they met with other members of their cult the following day, which they referred to as the Lord's Day. Usually those meetings were held in private homes.

We simply watched a few of those meetings the first Sunday after we received our assignment. We counted the number of people who gathered and discussed how we should proceed.

The following Sunday we met in a designated room in the temple's Royal Porch. Several temple guards had been ordered to go with us to show that we were acting under the authority of God's high priest.

After walking southwest from the temple for about fifteen minutes, we arrived at the first location we planned to raid. There we met with Aaron, who had been quietly watching outside the house. He confirmed that people of the Way were gathered inside.

I walked to the door of the house and knocked. When the door was opened by a middle-aged woman, one of the guards stepped forward and seized her. The rest of us entered the house.

"By the authority of the high priest of God Almighty, all of you are under arrest," I announced in a loud voice. The people assembled inside looked up with shocked expressions but offered little resistance. We bound their hands with ropes and herded them back to the temple, where they were placed in the temple prison.

Over the next several weeks, we raided several additional church meetings, and also dragged hundreds of people from their homes and businesses. The people who were arrested were questioned and sometimes tortured by the authorities until they revealed names and locations of other members of their church.

Our expeditions took us to neighboring towns around Jerusalem, and eventually into the provinces of Samaria and Galilee, although we had to coordinate with other Roman authorities in those regions.

After several months, I became convinced that we needed to go still farther. We had become aware that a sizeable contingent of Jesus' followers was in the Syrian city of Damascus. Although some were people who had lived in Damascus all their lives, many had fled there as a result of our persecution. I prayed about the matter at length, and became convinced that it was the Lord's will for me to go to Syria.

I therefore went to the high priest and asked for letters to the synagogues of Damascus allowing me to arrest any man or woman I found that belonged to the Way. Caiaphas gave me such a letter, and it authorized me to bring any such person back as a prisoner to Jerusalem. Attached to it was a Roman warrant for their arrests.

I found myself looking forward to persecuting Jesus' followers in Damascus. Little did I know how important that journey would actually be to me . . . or how radically it would change my life.

10.

Jonathan, three of my Cilician friends, and two temple guards accompanied me on our journey to Damascus. Because of the distance involved, we rode horses and took along a locking cage on a horse-drawn wagon.

We left the temple through the Sheep Gate about an hour before dawn, skirted the Fortress Antonia, and proceeded north along the Damascus Road. Pious Jews normally took the Jericho Road down into the Jordan River valley in order to avoid going through Samaria, but we didn't bother. Speed and stealth were more important to us than was prejudice against the half-breeds who largely populated Samaria.[11] Besides, by leaving as early as we did on horses, we hoped to be entirely through Samaria before nightfall.

We paused briefly in the Samaritan city of Sebaste, and then pressed on into Galilee. Although we had hoped to make it all the way to Capernaum that first day, we ended up spending the night near the Galilean town of Garis. The second day we were able to pass the Sea of Galilee and get to the highlands north of Lake Hula. We spent the night in Caesarea Philippi.

About noon on the third day, we were leisurely riding our horses along the road not quite twenty stadia[12] from Damascus, talking about our plans, when I was suddenly

---

[11] Samaritans were descended from Israelites who had intermarried with Gentiles the Assyrians brought in after they captured Samaria in 722 B.C.

[12] Approximately two miles.

enveloped by a bright light that seemed to emanate from heaven. I quickly halted my horse and looked around. The light was so bright I was unable to see my companions—or much else, for that matter.

"I may be having sunstroke," I gasped as I attempted to dismount. Jonathan rushed to my aid and helped me safely get off my horse.

"What's happening to me?" I asked as I fell to the ground.

A voice suddenly boomed in my ears. "Saul, Saul, why do you persecute me? It is hard for you to kick against the goads."[13]

I knew the voice had to be the Lord's—who else could know of my secret struggles as I *kicked against the goads* by mentally comparing and contrasting the legalism of Jewish law and Pharisaic rules with the radiance and joy evident in Stephen and other followers of Jesus—but it didn't make sense to me. I had been doing my best to fight *for* the Lord. In fact, I'd been sent out by God Almighty's duly appointed high priest. The idea that I could be persecuting God was absolutely repugnant to me.

"Who are you, Lord?" I asked. I desperately needed clarification.

"I am Jesus, whom you are persecuting," the voice responded. Jesus himself appeared in the midst of the blinding light. In fact, the blinding light appeared to be emanating from him. It was a transcendent and appealing

---

[13] Goads were traditional farming implements used to prod or guide oxen and other livestock which were pulling a plough or a cart. Their pointed ends made "kicking against the goads" an extremely unpleasant experience for the animal being goaded. Like a man driving an ox, the Holy Spirit had been driving Saul toward certain truths—but he had been resisting violently, *kicking against the goads* because he knew he had no answer for the arguments presented by Stephen and the other believers. At the same time, there were aspects of their arguments that Saul could not accept, and the conflict was a torment to him.

light that seemed to radiate from his powerful but loving face. As he gestured to me, I felt my barriers and walls of resistance breaking down and silently being swept aside.

I felt as if the light was drawing me in, pulling my life into that of the radiant being before me. Jesus seemed to be sifting through my startled mind, soothing my mental anguish and calming my troubled spirit. I was left with the exhilarating euphoria of being loved unreservedly . . . and with the sobering realization that I could never again persecute either him or his followers.

"Now get up and stand on your feet. I have appeared to you to appoint you as a servant and as a witness of what you have seen of me and what I will show you. Go into the city, and you will be told what you must do."

As the vision of Jesus faded from my sight, so did everything else. My eyes went from registering blinding light to an all-consuming darkness. I experienced momentary panic as I groped around me in complete blackness.

"Where are you?" I called franticly to my companions.

"We're here, Saul," Jonathan and Aaron answered together.

"What happened?" Aaron asked.

"I'm not sure," I responded. "Please tell me what you saw and heard, so I'll know I wasn't hallucinating or having sunstroke," I pleaded.

"I saw a bright light suddenly surround you and I heard some kind of noise, but I couldn't make it out," Aaron replied.

"Same here," added Jonathan, "except that the noise was almost like a voice—but I couldn't understand the words."

The other men responded similarly. Then they led me into Damascus. I was taken to the house of a well-known local merchant named Judas. A doctor was called, and he examined me. He applied some type of salve to my eyes, but it did no good.

At first my men were almost beside themselves trying to help me, but I was finally able to persuade them to go on about the city and see the sights.

"Please leave me alone for the time being," I requested. "I need to earnestly pray to make certain I know the Lord's will."

"But Saul," Jonathan protested. "We are here on the Lord's mission. What more do we need to know?"

"When I was blinded, the Lord told me he may have an entirely different mission for me. I need to pray until I know for certain what we are to do."

"Would you like for us to be rounding up Jesus' followers while you recuperate?"

"No, Jonathan," I answered. "I think it is important that I ascertain what God's will is before we do anything else. See the sights of the city. Enjoy yourselves. Let me fast and pray."

*****

They left me alone at the house of Judas in Damascus. Well, not really alone, since other members of Judas' household were there. But in another sense, I was more alone than I had ever been before, for I felt as if I were adrift in uncharted waters—abandoned by my religious moral compass that had directed me for so long. I thought I had been following hard after God's directive for my life, but the vision I had seen and heard showed me graphically that I had been wandering blindly in the wrong direction.

Now I truly am blind. With eyes wide open, I strained with all my might to make out details around me, but I could see nothing. The blackness of my vision became a metaphor to me for the darkness of my spiritual relationship with God. I had been trying to make sense of my predicament by mentally checking off those things I knew to be true facts, and then attempting to analyze what else I needed to know.

I had retraced my life history in an effort to see where I may have gone wrong, but I felt no closer to the enigma of how to extricate myself from my physical and spiritual darkness. Perhaps the problem was that I had been looking at my life from my perspective and my own training. Perhaps I needed to shift my focus, broaden my vision, and look at everything from a different perspective. *But how?*

I went to sleep that first night with questions swimming through my mind. I periodically awoke from a restless sleep with questions and riddles still prodding my consciousness. I felt as if I was falling out of control, flailing through a mystery wrapped in an enigma. But gradually certain questions emerged as being keys to the riddle.

Who are you, Lord? That had been my question on the road.

"I am Jesus, whom you are persecuting," the voice had responded.

I realized that I had accepted the fact that it was the Lord speaking to me, and it was the Lord who halted my activities with this blindness. The Lord apparently wanted me to grasp who he really was.

Who are you, Lord? The answer I received was that *Jesus is the Lord.*

But how can that possibly be true? Perhaps instead of analyzing my own life, what I really needed to analyze was what I knew to be true about God—and about Jesus.

At least twice each day, it was my custom to pray the words comprising the initial part of the *Shema Yisrael*: "Hear, O Israel: the Lord is our God; the Lord is one."[14] I believe there is one—and only one—God who created all else that exists, and it is that God whom I worship. But if there is only one God, then how could he have a son? Wouldn't that mean there would be more than one God?

---

[14] Deuteronomy 6:4; The Shema is typically comprised of Deuteronomy 6:4-9, 11:13-21, and Numbers 15:37-41.

Help me, Lord. If there is only one God, how can a man named Jesus also be Lord?

My thoughts involuntarily swirled back to a lesson taught by Gamaliel. My old teacher had been explaining the meanings of God's name to us. YHWH can mean either "I AM who I AM" or "I AM who I choose to be." Gamaliel concluded by telling us, "God is a spirit or spiritual force who can appear to us in any manner he chooses."

If God could appear as a burning bush, a pillar of fire, or an angel, could he also appear as a man named Jesus? *Probably—but why would he do so? What could be the purpose?*

Once again I realized I needed to shift my focus, broaden my vision, and look at everything from a different perspective. Not my perspective; not what I knew to be true; not even what I had seen or believed; I needed to see the problem from God's perspective.

11.

"Saul, please wake up. We have prepared breakfast for you."

"What?" I stammered. "Who's there?"

"Deborah. I'm the servant appointed by Judas and Hannah to look after you."

Judas, the Damascus merchant who is my host while I'm in town. Hannah is his wife; Deborah is one of their servants or slaves. My troubled mind must have finally allowed me to sleep after it concluded that I must see the problem from God's perspective. Maybe it just collapsed from the enormity of the problem. *How can a finite mind like mine ever hope to even gain a partial glimpse of God's infinite wisdom—much less of his perspective?*

"Sir, we have prepared breakfast for you," Deborah repeated.

"Oh, thank you," I said, as my thoughts regrouped. "I appreciate all you and your masters have done, but I feel that I must spend today fasting and praying."

"But you have not had anything to eat or drink since arriving yesterday afternoon. Wouldn't you like something? Anything?"

"You can lead me to where I need to go to relieve myself. But otherwise, I'm fine. Thank you."

I did consent to taking a few cups of water, but otherwise I ate and drank nothing. Instead, I spent my second day in Damascus fasting and praying earnestly to the

Lord. I hoped God would show me his way and his perspective, would answer my questions, and would lead me where he would have me go.

Minutes stretched into hours, and the hours dragged by as I continued to reach out to God in prayer. I knew that someone—probably Deborah—was occasionally checking on me, for my cup was periodically refilled with water. Twice I thought I heard the muffled voices of Jonathan and Aaron, though they did not address me directly. Everyone appeared to be willing to let me fast and pray as I had requested.

There were moments when I was seized with panic attacks. The darkness became so oppressive, so all-consuming, that I feared it would continue forever. *Lord, will I ever see again? What must I do to regain my sight?* But God let me sit in darkness with no answers to my questions, no direction clear for my way forward.

Eventually the background noises of the house stilled, and I assumed the members of the household had gone to their respective beds. I continued to pray, but felt I had many more questions than answers. My prayers gradually changed in their direction and scope. Instead of prying God with incessant questions, I moved toward asking that he show me the way, and I became more willing to follow—*follow blindly if need be, I thought wryly*—where God wanted to lead me.

I was rewarded with a vision. In my mind I saw a man with a well-cropped black beard hesitantly approaching me and laying hands on my head. The man had a kind face, though he appeared to be terrified of something. Although something seemed to be holding him back, he nevertheless stepped forward toward me, looked up toward heaven, and asked that my sight be restored. At that point, the vision stopped, but I felt that the Lord was telling me that I was about to have my sight restored, and that this unknown man was the key to answering my questions.

I also felt the presence of a message being implanted in my mind: *I will rescue you from your own people and from the Gentiles. I am sending you to them to open their eyes and turn them from darkness to light, and from the power of Satan to God, so that they may receive forgiveness of sins and a place among those who are sanctified by faith in me.*

I sat in the darkness and thanked God for the vision. I promised the Lord that if he would make the vision come true, I would go with that man wherever he led me and would earnestly endeavor to learn what I needed to know. If God had a purpose for my life, I would do my best to carry it out to the best of my ability. I would put my *blind trust* in my Creator, my God, my Master. *Lead me, Lord, where you would have me go. I am yours to command. From this moment forward, I am your bond slave.*

*****

I heard the knock at the door. I also noted the cessation of other sounds. Apparently the noise makers momentarily stopped their activities while confirming the sound.

More knocking. This time I heard someone hurrying past me. The door opened.

An unfamiliar man's voice asked, "Is Saul of Tarsus here?"

"Yes, sir." It sounded like Deborah's voice.

"It is imperative that I see him immediately."

"Follow me."

I heard footsteps approaching, slowing . . . and stopping. I thought of the vision I had seen earlier, and mentally merged the scene with the sounds I was hearing. In my mind I could picture the man with the cropped black beard silently gazing at me. He appeared to be frozen in abject terror as he first looked at me and then furtively glanced around as if unseen assailants might pounce upon him at any moment.

In my vision he had glanced up toward heaven and said a quick prayer. His hesitation seemed to confirm that mental picture. Then gathering his courage, he stepped forward toward the place where I sat silently on a mat.

I felt the man's hands lightly rest upon my head. No, make that one hand on my head and the other hand on my left shoulder. I heard him take a deep breath, release it, and then take another one.

"Brother Saul," he said, "the Lord Jesus has sent me to you. He is the same one who appeared to you along the road. He wants you to be able to see and to be filled with the Holy Spirit. I now ask God to restore your vision and show you his way."

The man paused briefly, squeezed my shoulder slightly, and proclaimed, "Brother Saul, receive your sight!"

Suddenly I felt as if something similar to fish scales was falling from my eyes, and I could see again. I got to my feet and looked around. I looked intently at the man who had helped me regain my sight.

"You're the man I saw in my vision!" I exclaimed.

"Yes, Saul—and you're the man I saw in *my* vision," he responded. "My name is Ananias, and I think you are supposed to come with me."

"I think I am, too."

A young woman stood in the doorway. I walked to her and said, "And you must be Deborah."

She merely nodded her head. I took her hands in mine and said, "Thank you for your kindness. Please tell Judas and Hannah I appreciate their taking me in and giving me a place to stay while I have been in Damascus. I hope I can repay them for their kindness and hospitality sometime. Thank you."

I turned, nodded to Ananias, and we left.

Perhaps it was my imagination or possibly just a new appreciation for coloration, but I found myself drinking in the sights that surrounded me. The colors seemed to be especially vibrant, and I had never seen things appear so sharp and well-defined. I marveled at the beauty that surrounded me and wondered if I had become overly accustomed to normal everyday vistas. *Has my blindness caused me to appreciate sights I had taken for granted, or has my vision been restored to be better than before? Whichever is true, Lord, thank you!*

As we walked along a street lined with Corinthian columns, I admired the way the brilliant white stones contrasted with the other colors of the shops, the sky, and even the people hustling through the city. It was just an ordinary scene—but after regaining my sight, it appeared extraordinary to me.

Ananias turned to me as we walked along and said, "The God of our fathers has chosen you to know his will and to see the Righteous One and to hear words from his mouth. You will be his witness to all men of what you have seen and heard."

He and I exchanged tales of our respective visions. He also told me about how dreams of my persecution had haunted his troubled sleep even before he had a vision telling him to find me and restore my sight. When we got to his house, Ananias opened the front door and called out, "Rachel?"

I heard the sound of feet running toward us and a pretty maiden who had apparently been crying rushed to Ananias and smothered him with an embrace and kisses.

"Oh, you made it back safely!" she exclaimed.

"Of course, Rachel. I told you the Lord would protect me and go with me."

"I know, but I was still afraid I would never see you again."

"There's someone I want you to meet."

"What?"

"There's someone you need to meet."

Ananias gently extricated himself from Rachel's embrace, stepped back through the doorway, and gestured toward me with his right hand.

"Rachel, I'd like you to meet Saul of Tarsus."

Rachel's eyes widened in terror and she shrank backward. At first Ananias didn't seem to notice, since he had turned toward me and was saying, "And this is my lovely wife, Rachel." As he turned back toward his wife, he saw her terrified expression.

I bowed slightly toward her and quietly said, "I'm sorry if my appearance has troubled you."

She said nothing, but her eyes were darting back and forth between Ananias and me.

Ananias gestured toward a couple of couches in the front room as he said to me, "Why don't you be seated and make yourself comfortable?" Turning to his wife, he added, "Would you please bring us a bowl of grapes?"

Rachel silently nodded.

"Thank you," he said.

"The Lord indicated to me that you have been fasting and praying while you have been here in Damascus," Ananias said as we reclined on the couches.

"That's correct."

"You've been here—what—three days?"

"Yes. This is the third day."

"With nothing to eat or drink during that entire time?"

"I had some water."

"You must be famished!"

"My soul was in turmoil; I needed to pray more than I needed to eat."

"Have you found the answers you were seeking, Saul?"

"Enough to know I was headed in the wrong direction. I now know that Jesus is Lord and I have committed myself to serve him. Not all my questions have been answered, but it will probably take an intensive study of scriptures and much additional prayer to get those answers."

"You say you have committed yourself to serve Jesus. Have you accepted him as your Lord and Savior?"

"What do you mean?"

"Do you admit that you are a sinner?"

"Most definitely."

"Have you repented of your sins and asked for God's forgiveness?"

"Yes."

"Have you accepted Christ as your personal savior?"

"What do you mean?"

"Under the old covenant, we were required to bring a blood sacrifice in order to gain atonement for our sins. God would accept the blood of the lamb as a substitute for the sinner's blood and would forgive the penitent sinner. Under God's new covenant with us, God . . ."

"Wait a minute, Ananias. What new covenant?"

"The new and better covenant instituted by Jesus when he came. Hundreds of years ago it was prophesied that the Messiah would usher in a new and better covenant. Under the new covenant, God provided the perfect sacrifice in Jesus, who willingly went to the cross to save us from our sinful nature. If we accept the blood sacrifice God made for us by claiming Jesus as our Lord and Savior, then we can have an everlasting relationship with God."

"Let me get this straight, Ananias. You're saying that Jesus' crucifixion was actually God's sacrifice for us to save us from our sinful nature?"

"Something like that, yes."

"And all I have to do is to accept it as a gift from God?"

"Well, you also have to realize that you are a sinner in need of God's mercy and forgiveness."

"That's obviously true."

"And you have to believe that Jesus is the Son of God and that he gave his life as a sacrifice for our sins."

"I think that's the part I'm having trouble with. If there is one—and only one—God who created all else, how can he have a son? Wouldn't that mean there is more than one God?"

"Remember that God is a spirit who can do whatever he chooses to do."

"Yes, and he can be whatever he chooses to be. That's one of the things Gamaliel taught us. One of the meanings of the name God chose for himself—*YHWH*—is 'I AM who I choose to be.'"

"That's right, Saul. In order to provide the perfect sacrifice for us, it was necessary for God to take part of his spirit, and use it to become a human who was able to live among us and be tempted as we are—but yet not yield to those temptations. Since Jesus is God in human form, he could live a sinless life, thus becoming the perfect sacrifice for our sins. But he was also human, limited by being subject to the dimensions of the universe God created—which meant he could die. Do you understand what I am saying, Saul?"

"I think so . . . and I think that was a large part of what I needed to have explained to me."

"Why don't you pray about it some more while I visit with Rachel? She needs to hear about your transformation."

"Thank you. I'd like that."

I prayed—but I also thought about what Ananias had said. He had claimed that Jesus was God in human form—come to Earth to be the perfect sacrifice for our sins. His words seemed to swirl around in my mind. I fought for clarity and understanding. *Help me, Lord. Are Ananias' words true and correct? Is it possible that the Messiah came to be God's redeeming sacrifice rather than to be God's eternal king? Or is he both? Give me insight and clarity, Lord!*

Gradually another scene forced its way to the forefront of my memory. Gamaliel and I were walking back toward Jerusalem after we had gone to the Jordan River to see John the Baptist. My old teacher had admitted to me that his teaching had largely skipped some of the messianic prophesies that seemed to be at odds with the ones portraying the Christ as an everlasting king who would rule his people forever—not because he didn't believe them, but rather because he wasn't sure how all the prophesies fit together.

What was it he had said to me at that time?

The scene suddenly became clear in my memory. Gamaliel turned to me, looked me in the eye, and remarked, "We generally think of the Messiah as being the great king who will sit on his ancestor David's throne and rule his people forever. Right?"

Yes.

"But the most detailed messianic prophesy we have comes from Isaiah, who spoke of how his kingdom would never end. But Isaiah also wrote about the Messiah being a suffering servant who would be beaten and bruised for our sins. The two pictures don't seem to jibe. Also, Daniel says the Messiah will be cut off or killed. Cut off from what? Killed? How does that fit in with a king who will rule his people forever?"

Oh, God! I suddenly understand! Your word has told us all along that the promised Messiah will actually be your perfect sacrifice . . . for us. You loved us so much that you did that for us? I prostrated myself on the floor and wept as the enormity of God's love overwhelmed me.

Then I pieced together the implications. The scriptures consistently tell us that God is a spirit and that he can take whatever form he chooses and can be who he chooses to be. If God used a part of his own spirit to become human, there would not really be two separate gods. Rather, part of God's spirit would simply exist in human form.

But why would he need to do it that way?

Since God is eternal, he cannot die. But a sacrifice *would have to die.* The Messiah would have to be cut off or killed in order to save us from our sins. On the other hand, he would also have to be raised from the dead in order to reign over his people forever. The prophesies were not really at odds, after all. Rather, they were two sides of the same coin!

The more I thought about it, the more comfortable I was with my conclusions—and the more excited I became. Now when I prayed, my prayers were no longer blocked by mental battlegrounds of conflicting thoughts and emotions. Rather, I found I could praise God with elation and joy that had been sorely missing, and could honestly seek the Master's will and direction. Prayer became less a mental exercise and more a time of fellowship with the Supreme Intelligence of the universe. For me, it was a wonderful awakening into a brave new world filled with possibilities and potential.

12.

I made it a practice to worship in the local Jewish synagogue wherever I might be on the Sabbath. The rabbi of the local synagogue would customarily invite any visiting rabbi who might be attending the service to come forward and read from the scroll that had been chosen for that day's scripture reading. Since I was a member of the Sanhedrin of Jerusalem, I knew the local rabbi would almost certainly call on me to teach from the chosen Scripture.

I therefore got up early on the Sabbath, washed and dressed, and then spent much time in prayer. *Oh Lord, if I am to speak, please guide the selection of scripture so that it is what you wish to be taught, fill me with your Holy Spirit, and help me to say what you want me to say.*

I walked to the synagogue with Ananias and Rachel. Ananias was pleasant, courteous, and somewhat more talkative than usual. I suspected he was attempting to get Rachel to relax and be more comfortable. *At least she no longer looks like a terrified rabbit caught in a snare; I suppose that's progress.*

I turned to Ananias and remarked, "Don't you think this is a bit ironic?"

His puzzled expression showed he did not grasp my meaning.

"You know," I prompted. "My going to the synagogue with you. After all, this *is* the same synagogue I had planned to attend today in order to arrest Jesus' followers."

"Now, instead of arresting us, you are coming with us."

I noticed that the conversation was not helping Rachel to relax. I put my arm around Ananias and said, "Not only that, but I have made a profession of faith and you have even baptized me!"

"Fellow believers in the Lord Jesus Christ," Ananias remarked.

"My brother and sister in Christ," I said. At last all three of us smiled.

*****

Ananias introduced me to the leader of the Damascus synagogue, Rabbi Benjamin, who asked me if I would be willing to briefly teach part of the lesson, which would be from Isaiah.

"I would be most honored," I replied.

I had conflicting emotions when I caught sight of Jonathan and Aaron at the synagogue. We had come to Damascus on a mission that we thought was for God: to seize, arrest, and persecute the followers of Jesus. But then Jesus himself had appeared to me and had given me a radically different mission. How would my old friends view my defection from their cause? I didn't have to wait long to find out; Jonathan made his way through the crowd to where I stood.

"I see you have your sight back."

"Yes; it has been restored."

"Deborah told us some man came to the house, asked for you, and she took him to you. She said he laid his hands on you and you were cured."

"That's essentially correct."

"So, what do we do now? Are you ready to proceed with our mission?"

"No. The mission has been changed."

"Tell me about it."

"Do you remember the bright light that blinded me while we were on the road here?"

"Yes."

"The light that surrounded me was radiating from the Lord himself. Do you remember telling me later that you heard something that sounded like a voice, but you couldn't make out the words?"

"Yes."

"The Lord was speaking directly to me."

"What did he say?"

"He asked me why I was persecuting him."

"That's crazy. We weren't persecuting him," Jonathan protested. "We have been persecuting the people who have been blaspheming his name. In fact, we have been commissioned by his very own high priest to do it!"

"I know, Jonathan. That's why I've spent so much time praying these past several days."

"Has it helped?"

"Yes. I can see much more clearly now—both physically and spiritually."

Our conversation was interrupted as Rabbi Benjamin began the Sabbath service with recitation of the *Mincha* prayers and accompanying psalms. We quietly took our seats and recited the prayers and psalms. The rabbi read to us from the Torah, and we all joined in prayer.

Then he turned to the congregation and said, "It has come to my attention that we have with us today a visiting rabbi who is also a member of the Great Sanhedrin in Jerusalem. We would be most honored if Saul, formerly of Tarsus, will read and teach us from the writings of Isaiah."

I slowly rose to my feet and walked to the front, where a scroll was spread across the *bimah*. I read the following passage aloud:

> For to us a child is born,
> To us a son is given,
> And the government will be on his shoulders.
> And he will be called
> Wonderful Counselor, Mighty God,
> Everlasting Father, Prince of Peace.
> Of the increase of his government and peace
> There will be no end.
> He will reign on David's throne

> And over his kingdom,
> Establishing and upholding it
> With justice and righteousness
> From that time on and forever.
> The zeal of the Lord God Almighty
> Will accomplish this.[15]

I took a breath as I looked at the people assembled in the room, bowed slightly to Benjamin, and said, "This is one of the messianic prophesies written by Isaiah. We are all familiar with the last portion of this passage, since we eagerly and earnestly await the coming of the Anointed One who 'will reign on David's throne and over his kingdom, establishing and upholding it with justice and righteousness from that time on and forever.'

"Because we chafe under the rule of foreign governments, we tend to look for a mighty military leader. But look at the attributes Isaiah says the Messiah will have. Listen to the titles he is given: Wonderful Counselor, Mighty God, Everlasting Father, and Prince of Peace.

"We go to a counselor for advice, especially in troubled times. How many of you have a troubled heart? How many have cried out to God for help, for advice, for guidance? How many of you could use a wonderful counselor about now? I know I needed one this past week.

"Some of you may know me by reputation. I have been hunting down followers of Jesus of Nazareth. In fact, I was on my way here to Damascus to arrest wonderful and caring people like Ananias and Rachel. I thought I was doing God's will and carrying out his mission. After all, I had letters of authority from God's high priest himself!

"When I was a few stadia from Damascus, a bright light from heaven blinded me and caused me to fall to the

---

[15] Isaiah 9:6-7.

ground. A voice from heaven asked me, 'Saul, Saul, why are you persecuting me?' 'Who are you, Lord?' I asked. The voice replied, 'I am Jesus, whom you are persecuting.' When I looked into the blinding light, I saw Jesus himself! In fact, the light seemed to be radiating from him.

"Have you ever had facts turn out to be totally different from what you expected? That's when you need a wonderful counselor! I found mine this week when I spent several days fasting and praying—and I'm here to tell you that you can have that same counselor helping you.

"Look at the next two titles for the Messiah. Isaiah said he would be called both the Mighty God and the Everlasting Father or Father of all eternity. Think about it. Those are terms that are reserved for God alone—yet the greatest of all our prophets said the Messiah would be called those titles. The Messiah is a man. We call it blasphemy if a man claims to be God or makes himself equal to God. Yet Isaiah spoke glowingly of terms reserved for God alone being used to describe the Messiah. Why wouldn't that be blasphemy?"

I looked over the crowd. All were looking at me intently, but no one answered.

"Why wouldn't that be blasphemy?" I repeated.

Still no answer.

"Listen to the last sentence of the passage I read to you: 'The zeal of the Lord God Almighty will accomplish this.' Isaiah himself gave us the answer: If it is God himself who does it, how can it be blasphemy?"

"Think about it. The mighty God who created the universe—the Everlasting Father of all eternity—came to earth not only to be the promised Messiah, but also to save us from our sins and to redeem us unto himself so that we can have an eternal relationship with him. This is the good news Isaiah promised in the scriptures I read to you today.

"Finally, Isaiah says the Messiah will be called the Prince of Peace. Do you need peace in your life? Are you tired of the turmoil and chaos? Have you done your best to follow the letter of God's law, but have found it to be unfulfilling and unsatisfying? Do you long to have a real relationship with the loving God who created you and loves you more than you can possibly imagine? Let God's Messiah bring you peace that passes all understanding. That's his job. After all, he is the Prince of Peace."

Nodding to the rabbi again, I returned to my seat.

Rabbi Benjamin rose, walked slowly to the *bimah*, looked down at the scroll containing Isaiah's words, and then looked silently at the people seated in front of him. He appeared to be at a loss for words.

Finally he choked out a broken sentence in halting fashion. "I . . . I don't know when . . . I have ever heard anything that . . . startled me as much as . . . as what I have just heard."

He took a deep breath before continuing. "I sense that many of you may have questions you may wish to ask our guest . . . and anything I have to say may be rather trite by comparison. Therefore, let us stand and be dismissed. Please join me in the Priestly Blessing:

> The Lord bless you and keep you;
> The Lord make his face shine upon you
> And be gracious to you;
> The Lord turn his face toward you and give you peace.[16]
> *Shalom.*"

"I would like to visit with you in a more private setting sometime this next week if you don't mind," Benjamin said after the benediction.

"I would like that," I responded.

The rabbi and I bowed slightly to each other, and then he retreated to visit with others in the synagogue.

---

[16] Numbers 6:22-26.

Ananias introduced me to several of his friends, though they were understandably guarded—possibly even suspicious—when around me.

I noticed that my older friends with whom I had journeyed to Damascus were standing apart and eyeing me with even greater suspicion. Some of the men who were with them had looks of open hostility or anger.

*****

"All right, Saul," Jonathan said later after most of the people had left. He and my Cilician friends were huddled around me so that we could talk privately. "Tell me straight. What are you up to?"

"Nothing. What I said was precisely what happened—and is what I believe to be the truth."

"You mean this isn't simply a ruse to get in with Jesus' followers?"

"No, Jonathan. Jesus actually appeared to me while we were on the road to Damascus. While I was blind, he sent me a vision of Ananias laying his hands on my head and restoring my sight—and he sent a similar vision to Ananias commanding him to do so at Judas' house on Straight Street."

"I was with you when you were blinded, Saul. You said at the outset that you thought you might be having a sunstroke." Jonathan held me at arm's length as he looked steadily into my eyes. "Are you sure you didn't simply get overheated?"

"I'm sure . . ."

I paused momentarily and then added, "Think about it, Jonathan. Have you ever known anyone more dedicated toward persecuting Jesus' followers than I have been?"

"I've never known anyone who was more dedicated than you about anything, Saul."

"The Lord had to personally intervene to cause me to change directions like that."

"Maybe so . . ."

"It is so!"

"You mean to tell me that Jesus is the Messiah?"

"Yes."

"What about being disqualified because he had been crucified? You know, that business about anyone who was hung on a tree being under God's curse?"

"Well, Jesus *was* under God's curse—but not just because he was hung upon a tree. The biggest reason he was under God's curse is that he took the sins of the world on his shoulders when he died in our place as a sacrifice for our sins."

"As you yourself pointed out earlier, Saul, how can Jesus be God's Messiah if he is under God's curse?"

"Don't you see, Jonathan?" I asked, taking his hands in mine and looking into his eyes. "The Messiah's primary mission was to pay the debt for our sins by becoming the perfect sacrifice for those sins. By dying on the cross, Jesus took the penalty for our sins upon himself, paid the debt in full, and set us free!"

"No, I don't see it, Saul. Maybe I could if I worked through scripture with you—but right now, it just doesn't add up for me."

"Would that be all right?" Aaron asked.

The rest of us looked at Aaron with blank expressions.

"Would what be all right?" I finally asked.

"If we could work through the scriptures with you. You were our teacher in Tarsus. I've learned more from you than I have anywhere else. I can tell you've had a life changing experience, and I want to learn more about it. Would that be all right?"

I just looked at Aaron without speaking. Then I looked at my other friends. They were all studying me intently, hopeful enthusiasm radiating from their expressions. Finally I asked, "Is that what the rest of you want as well?"

They all nodded.

"Wait for me outside. Let me see what I can do."

I turned and walked back across the room to where Rabbi Benjamin was standing.

"You said you wanted to talk to me," I said.

"Yes, Saul. I obviously know you by reputation—but your statements here today totally took me by surprise. I am intrigued by what you say happened to you and would like to visit with you about it in greater detail, if you don't mind."

"I would be most honored to do so. Would you prefer to visit privately or with others around?"

"Privately, I think. At least at first."

"Fine. Tell me a time and place, and I'll make it a point to be there. Also, is there a place where some friends and I can study the scriptures without being disturbed?"

Benjamin thought for a moment before answering. "Yes, meet me back here two days from now at this same time. I'll need to check with someone. If he approves our coming, I'll take you to a place where we can meet. It should also serve as a suitable place for you and your friends to study without being disturbed."

*****

Two days later I met Benjamin at the synagogue. He asked me to come with him. We walked to a simple mud brick house a couple of blocks away. Benjamin opened the front door, looked around, and then motioned for me to enter. The floor was hard-packed dirt mixed with clay, ash, and straw so that it was as hard as the mud brick walls.

Four wooden chairs faced each other toward the center of the room around a simple wood table. Mats for reclining were stacked against one wall, as were a couple of stools. The chairs had basic sycamore frames with woven-reed backs and seats, but their careful construction indicated that they were well made by a carpenter who took pride in their craftsmanship. I looked questioningly at Benjamin and remarked, "It's unusual to find this much furniture—especially of this quality—in such a simple structure."

"This house is actually owned by a wealthy friend who has made it exclusively available to us for however long you and your friends wish to use it for your studies," the rabbi replied. "He furnished it for your anticipated needs, and is willing to provide other items or even other accommodations if you need them. I have scrolls you can borrow."

"Which scrolls?"

"The Torah, the Psalms, and most of the prophets."

"Thank you. That would be a big help. Would you care to join us?"

"Not now. I might at some future time. Right now, I just want to visit with you about what happened on the road to Damascus."

"It happened just as I said earlier."

"You're certain that it was Jesus himself you saw and heard?"

"Absolutely. I had met him on a number of occasions in Jerusalem—but the meeting I will remember to my dying day is the one on the road here."

"And he asked why you were persecuting him?"

"That's right . . . and he said it is hard for me to kick against the goads."

"What did he mean by that?

"I'm not sure—but I think it may have had to do with the questions that had been raging in my mind ever since I heard Stephen's defense and saw his radiant expression and peace even while being murdered."

"Murdered? I thought he had been convicted by the Sanhedrin."

"We never took a vote. Even if we had voted, it probably would not have been legal, since we failed to follow our own law. I tried to sweep my objections aside and bury them in the frantic activity of persecuting Jesus' followers— but God knows my thoughts . . . and he knows my activities were merely useless kicking against the goads."

"Did Jesus say anything else to you?

"Yes. He said he was appointing me to be his servant and to be a witness of what I had seen and been told. He told me to go into Damascus and I would be told what I must do."

"So that's what you did?"

"I had no choice. When the light radiating from Jesus faded from view, so did everything else. I could see nothing for three days."

"What did you do?"

"I was taken to the house of Judas the merchant, and spent my time fasting and praying."

"Did you get the answers you were seeking?"

"Enough to know I had been wrong about Jesus and his followers. Enough to know I had been heading in the wrong direction. You might say God got my attention and turned me around."

Rabbi Benjamin nodded, smiled, and said, "That's the thing that has most impressed me about the people who have accepted Jesus as their—what do they call it?—their Savior? Their lives seem to be genuinely changed. Most of them seem to have a joy that's almost infectious. And a peace and contentment I have longed for—but haven't found."

"A peace that passes all understanding?"

"Exactly. That's what you called it on the Sabbath. You pointed out that Isaiah called the Messiah the Prince of Peace—and you asked if we were tired of the turmoil and chaos. I know I'm tired of it. I long for the peace you say you've found."

"Are you ready to accept Jesus as your Lord and Savior?"

"No. Not yet, anyway. In fact, I'd appreciate it if you would keep our conversation confidential for the time being."

"Certainly, Benjamin. I'll respect your wishes. Is that also the reason you'd rather not meet with the others for our searches through the scriptures?"

"Yes. Others in my synagogue look to me for answers. It would be better if you are the only one who knows I'm also searching. However, I would like to continue meeting with you privately, if you don't mind."

"I'd like that. Are you certain it's all right with the owner of this place for us to use it?"

"Yes. Hafid owns many properties in and around Damascus. This is one he is currently not using. It has the advantage of being near the synagogue, which makes it easier to transport the scrolls for your studies. Hafid also offered to provide lodging for you if you need it."

"Thank you. I'll keep that in mind."

13.

"Jonathan, Gamaliel taught us about the distinction between Jew and Gentile, and the reasons God had chosen us to be his special people. Do you remember?" I asked as I gathered with my friends who had accompanied me to Damascus.

"Do I ever!" he exclaimed. "He liked to put each of us on the spot—but it really helped to make us think."

"Do you remember the primary point he wanted us to learn from that exercise?"

"Yes. We are God's special covenant nation."

"And what was the covenant?"

"God made a covenant with Abraham that Isaac's descendants would be the channel by which God would bless all the peoples on earth."

"Very good," I said. "I borrowed some scrolls so that we could begin our study by looking at the covenant God made with his people. The scroll containing the entire Torah is kept in a special place at the synagogue, but Rabbi Benjamin allowed me to borrow a smaller scroll that contains Genesis." I read this passage aloud:

>The Lord had said to Abram,
>"Leave your country, your people and your father's household
>And go to the land I will show you.
>I will make you into a great nation and I will bless you;
>I will make your name great, and you will be a blessing.
>I will bless those who bless you,
>And whoever curses you I will curse;
>And all peoples on earth will be blessed through you."[17]

"Abram did what God asked. He left his home in Ur, went first to Haran and then on to the land of Canaan. Four

---

[17] Genesis 12: 1-3.

years later God changed Abram's name to Abraham and renewed his covenant:

> As for me, this is my covenant with you:
> You will be the father of many nations.
> No longer will you be called Abram; your name will be Abraham,
> For I have made you a father of many nations.
> I will make you very fruitful;
> I will make nations of you, and kings will come from you.
> I will establish my covenant as an everlasting covenant
> Between me and you and your descendants after you
> For the generations to come,
> To be your God and the God of your descendants after you.
> The whole land of Canaan, where you are now an alien,
> I will give as an everlasting possession
> To you and your descendants after you;
> And I will be their God.[18]

"God later tested Abraham by commanding him to sacrifice Isaac—his only son by his wife, Sarah—on top of Mount Moriah. Abraham obeyed the Lord's command and took Isaac to the top of the mountain," I said as I found the relevant scripture.

> When they reached the place God had told him about,
> Abraham built an altar there and arranged the wood on it.
> He bound his son Isaac and laid him on the altar,
> On top of the wood.
> Then he reached out his hand and took the knife to slay his son.
> But an angel of the LORD called out to him from heaven,
> "Abraham! Abraham!"
> "Here I am," he replied.
> "Do not lay a hand on the boy," he said.

---

[18] Genesis 17: 4-8. Abram means *exalted father,* while Abraham means *father of many.*

"Do not do anything to him. Now I know that you fear God,
Because you have not withheld from me your son, your only son."
Abraham looked up and there in a thicket
He saw a ram caught by its horns.
He went over and took the ram and sacrificed it as a burnt offering
Instead of his son.
So Abraham called that place *The LORD Will Provide*.
And to this day it is said,
"On the mountain of the LORD it will be provided."
The angel of the LORD
Called to Abraham from heaven a second time
And said, "I swear by myself, declares the LORD,
That because you have done this
And have not withheld your son, your only son,
I will surely bless you and make your descendants
As numerous as the stars in the sky
And as the sand on the seashore.
Your descendants will take possession of the cities of their enemies,
And through your offspring all nations on earth will be blessed,
Because you have obeyed me."[19]

"Isaac grew up and had two sons, Jacob and Esau. The LORD later appeared to Jacob in a dream or vision and told him:

I am the LORD,
The God of your father Abraham and the God of Isaac.
I will give you and your descendants the land on which you are lying.
Your descendants will be like the dust of the earth,
And you will spread out to the west and to the east,
To the north and to the south.
All peoples on earth will be blessed through you and your offspring.[20]

---

[19] Genesis 22: 9-18.

"What do the various covenants God made have in common with each other?" I asked.

"God promised his blessings upon Abraham, Isaac, Jacob and their descendants," Jonathan said.

"He compared their numbers to the stars in the sky, the sands on the shore, and the dust of the earth," added Aaron.

"God promised that he would give this land to them and their descendants," Michael said after a brief pause.

"And all peoples of the earth will be blessed through them and their offspring," Aaron added.

"I can see how having this land could constitute a blessing for the large numbers of descendants God promised the patriarchs," I said. "But how does that translate into being a blessing for all the peoples on earth?"

Silence.

"Isn't that part of God's covenant with his people?" I prodded.

Still no answer.

I looked into the eyes of each of my friends until they glanced elsewhere or otherwise averted my gaze. Finally Michael stammered, "Wh—what do you mean?"

"Think about it. Part of God's covenant with his people is that all the peoples of the earth will be blessed through the children of Israel. How can that be?"

"Could it be through the promised Messiah?" Aaron eventually ventured.

I looked at each of my friends in turn and waited to see if anyone had anything else to add. None of them did. Finally I grinned slightly, nodded and said, "That's what I think, too."

"Why?" asked Jonathan.

---

[20] Genesis 28: 13-14.

"I strongly suspect that God had at least a couple of major reasons for picking Abraham's descendants through Isaac and Jacob to be his chosen people. First, in a world of false religions of people worshiping various gods that represented different aspects of God's creation, God could directly interact with one nation that would know him, his laws, and his commandments. That would be the shorter-term goal or objective.

"The second and longer-term objective involved preparing the way for the Messiah, the coming of the Messiah, and the blessing of all peoples through the work of the Messiah. I suggest that we go through the Psalms and the writings of various prophets to see what the scriptures say about the promised Messiah."

"How does that differ from what you and I have already done with Gamaliel?" Jonathan asked.

"Gamaliel once told me that he had purposely avoided some of the major prophesies about the Anointed One because he thought they contradicted some of the other prophesies concerning the Messiah. I propose that we look at everything we can find that the prophets said about the Christ—even if some of the passages appear to be contradictory."

"Sounds good to me," said Aaron. The others nodded in agreement.

14.

"Let's review the prophecies of the Messiah that we have seen these past few weeks as we studied the scrolls of the Psalms and the writings of Isaiah," I said to my friends a few weeks later. "Remember that since Psalms are poems that are generally set to music and sung, they typically are written from the point of view of the singer and will not specifically mention the Messiah by name or title. Therefore, we have to be on the lookout for phrases that appear to address the future Anointed One whom God would send as a king or sacrifice.

"For example, the psalm that begins 'My God, my God, why have you forsaken me?'[21] indicates that the Messiah would be scorned, despised, mocked, and insulted. He would be encircled by a band of evil men who would pierce his hands and feet, would divide his garments and would cast lots for his clothing."

"It also says he would thirst," Aaron pointed out.

"Right you are," I replied. "We also read psalms that said that he would be betrayed by a close friend whom he trusted and with whom he had shared bread,[22] that none of his bones would be broken,[23] and that God would not abandon him to the grave or allow his body to decay.[24]"

"Those are the psalms I think refer to the Messiah. Does anyone else have any others?"

---

[21] Psalm 22.
[22] Psalm 41:9.
[23] Psalm 34:20.
[24] Psalm 16:10.

No one answered. I waited a few moments and then said, "All right, then. Which writings of Isaiah do you think may refer to the Messiah?"

"Well, there's the writing you read for us at the synagogue that first week we were in Damascus," Aaron answered. "You know, the one that says, 'For to us a child is born, to us a son is given, and the government will be on his shoulders. And he will be called wonderful counselor, mighty God, everlasting Father, and the prince of peace.'"[25]

"Don't forget that it also says that there will be no end of the increase of his government and peace, and that he will reign on David's throne and over his kingdom, establishing and upholding it with justice and righteousness from that time on and forever,"[26] Jonathan added.

"Very good," I remarked. "Immediately before that passage, Isaiah also tells us that he would be from (or live in) Galilee, and that he would be a light to people walking in darkness.[27] Later Isaiah says that he will be a light for the Gentiles so that God's salvation may spread throughout the earth."[28]

"Doesn't Isaiah also say he would be born of a virgin[29] and would be preceded by a voice from the desert to prepare the way for the Lord?"[30] Michael asked.

"Yes, Michael. You are absolutely correct," I responded.

"The one I especially liked called him the branch from the root of Jesse and said he will have the spirit of the Lord, as well as wisdom, understanding, power and peace,"[31] Jonathan said.

---

[25] Isaiah 9:6.
[26] Isaiah 9:7.
[27] Isaiah 9:1-2.
[28] Isaiah 49:6-7; 52:10.
[29] Isaiah 7:14.
[30] Isaiah 40:3-5.
[31] Isaiah 11:1-10.

"Isaiah also goes into great detail about how the Messiah would suffer as God's sacrifice for our sins," I said. "For example, Isaiah says he would be beaten, mocked and spat upon;[32] disfigured,[33] despised and rejected, pierced for our transgressions, and crushed for our iniquities. He would be silent like a sacrificial lamb, and would bear the sins of many, making intercession for them. He would be buried in a rich man's grave. His punishment brings peace for us.[34] His salvation will last forever, and his righteousness will never fail.[35] Does anyone remember any other Messianic prophesy by Isaiah?"

"Well, my notes indicate that Isaiah also said the Messiah would be a sure foundation, with justice and righteousness,"[36] Aaron said.

"Very good," I remarked. "Next time we will look at some passages in the writings of Jeremiah and Ezekiel."

I said a brief prayer for my friends and then they departed. I was still gathering up my notes and the scrolls I needed to return to Benjamin when Aaron quietly slipped back into the room.

"Oh, hello..." I began—but Aaron motioned for me to be quiet.

"Shhhh," he whispered. "I've got to tell you something important, but the others can't know that I'm doing it."

"Wha...."

"Shhhh. I overheard Jonathan making plans with some of the local Jews to arrest you and take you back to Jerusalem."

"When is this supposed to happen?"

---

[32] Isaiah 50:6.
[33] Isaiah 52:14.
[34] Isaiah 53.
[35] Isaiah 51:6.
[36] Isaiah 28:16-17.

"I didn't hear that part, but it sounded as if it would be very soon. You probably need to get out of town to a place of safety."

"Thanks, Aaron. But I really thought Jonathan was one of my closest friends."

"I think he likes you personally, but he also thinks you betrayed the cause."

"What do you think?"

"I think you are the most knowledgeable and dedicated person I've ever known. You wouldn't have converted to being a follower of Jesus unless that experience you told us about was real. Personally, I want to keep studying with you if it's at all possible—but I need to make sure you're safe first."

"What about the others that came with us from Cilicia?"

"I don't know for certain where they stand."

"Thank you, my friend, for the warning."

"You are most welcome, Saul."

After Aaron slipped back out the door, I sat in the room for several minutes thinking and praying about what I should do and where I should go. I then bundled up the scrolls and my notes and went to the synagogue, where I met Rabbi Benjamin.

"Thank you for letting me borrow these scrolls," I said.

"It was my pleasure, Saul."

"Several weeks ago you mentioned to me that the wealthy man who allowed us to use that house for our studies also said he could provide lodging for me if I needed it."

"Yes, that's true."

"Is that offer still open?"

"As far as I know, it is. Do you desire it now?"

"Yes. I just received a warning that I may be about to be arrested and taken back to Jerusalem."

"Come with me to my house. You can hide there while I check with Hafid to make certain the offer is still open. Are you still living with Ananias and Rachel?"

"Yes."

"I'll get word to them so they can move to a place of safety for the time being."

"Thank you."

Benjamin left me in a back room at his house while he visited with his wealthy friend. *Rabbi Benjamin is a Jewish religious leader*, I thought to myself. *Could he be in on the plot to arrest me? I think he's my friend—but then again, I thought Jonathan was also my friend. Whom can I trust?* I reflected for a few minutes, and then realized I knew the answer to that question. *I can trust the Lord.* I prayed and turned the matter over to God.

15.

My prayers were interrupted when Rabbi Benjamin returned with a fairly elderly man he identified as Erasmus, the trusted servant and assistant to Hafid. Since the two men had ridden horses back to Benjamin's house, I mounted the one that the rabbi had ridden and rode with Erasmus back to his master's villa, which was constructed of white and light brown stones on a ridge overlooking Damascus.

We dismounted at the stables adjacent to the main house, put the horses in their stalls, and entered the villa. Hafid and his wife, Lisha, were waiting for us on a covered porch that flanked an attractive garden. The city of Damascus spread out below us.

"I have heard much about you," Hafid said as he motioned me to a couch near the ones on which he and Lisha reclined.

"Oh, really?"

"Yes. You made quite a stir with your persecution of the people who believe Jesus is the Jewish Messiah. I had heard you had come to Damascus to round up more of Jesus' followers. Then I heard that you yourself had become a follower. Is this true?"

"Yes. You seem to have accurate sources of information."

"Having reliable channels of information has always been important to me—but I still prefer to go to the original source whenever possible. Please tell me about your conversion experience."

I told Hafid and Lisha about my encounter with Jesus on the road to Damascus, the visions Ananias and I had of each other, and my experiences since then. I thanked them for allowing me to use the small house they owned near Benjamin's synagogue for my teaching sessions, and told them about the warning I had received that I was about to be arrested by some of the Jewish religious authorities. Erasmus reappeared with bowls of cut fruit, which he put next to our respective couches. The break in conversation allowed me to once again admire the view we had of the city.

"You are most welcome to stay here with us as long as you desire to do so. Rabbi Benjamin has volunteered to bring whichever scrolls you wish to study, and I have a place here where you can meet with him or with others you think you can trust."

"Thank you. I appreciate your hospitality."
*****

I was sorely tempted to attend a worship service in Damascus—perhaps at a different synagogue—on the Sabbath, but was talked out of any such foolishness by Hafid, who advised me to quietly remain at his villa. I worshiped by praying and continuing my readings in the scrolls of Jeremiah's writings.

Jeremiah referred to the Messiah as being "the righteous branch descended from David" and said he would be called the LORD Our Righteousness.[37] However, the prophesy I found most intriguing was when the LORD said that the time is coming when he would make a new and better everlasting covenant that would be written on the people's hearts[38] rather than on stone.[39]

Two days later Rabbi Benjamin brought the scroll containing Ezekiel's writings to Hafid's house, and we were able to visit privately.

"Jonathan showed up at the synagogue with your friends from Cilicia. However, he also had some other men

---

[37] Jeremiah 22:5-6, 33:15-16.
[38] i.e., on their innermost being.
[39] Jeremiah 31:31-35.

with him whom I did not recognize . . . and they seemed especially anxious to find you. They asked if I had seen you."

"What did you say?"

"I told them I saw you the preceding Sabbath, but had not seen you this Sabbath."

"Did that satisfy them?"

"Not entirely. They continued to quiz others at the synagogue, but no one seemed to know where you were."

"What about Ananias and Rachel?"

"I went to their house immediately after you left with Erasmus to come here. I warned them to leave for the time being. They said they had been thinking about visiting Rachel's parents in Caesarea, and thought this might be just the time to do so."

"That's good. I would hate for them to be arrested just because they were so gracious and caring to me."

We sat in silence for several minutes before I eventually muttered, "So, it appears the warning was correct and timely, after all . . ."

"I would say so, Saul."

"Although I am glad I was able to escape to safety, I am also rather sad Jonathan tried to betray me."

"Yes, friendships are precious things that should be treasured. It comes as a bitter shock when a friend turns his back on you or otherwise tramples on your relationship."

"That it does, Benjamin. That it does. I also miss being with Aaron, Michael and John, my three friends from Cilicia who came with me to Damascus."

"Would you like for me to check on them and try to ascertain their feelings and motives?"

"That would be nice. I hope they are still faithful friends."

*****

Aaron and Michael accompanied Benjamin when he brought me the scroll of Daniel's writings two weeks later.

"Shalom, Saul!" Aaron beamed as he greeted me. "It is wonderful to know that you are still safe and sound!"

"Shalom," I answered. "It is good to see both of you again."

"I have been quietly visiting with Aaron and Michael over the past couple of weeks, and we decided that a change in their lodging would be appropriate," Benjamin explained.

I looked questioningly at all three men.

"Jonathan has gone back to Jerusalem, John has returned to Tarsus, and we felt out of place where we were," Aaron explained.

"Yes. Both of us wanted to learn more scripture from you if we could, but we weren't even sure you were still in this area," Michael added. "At first, no one seemed to know where you were, but yesterday Rabbi Benjamin told us to meet him at the house where we had studied with you earlier."

"I told them I could lead them to you if that is what they really wanted," Benjamin said.

"Hafid said they could stay here and study scripture with you as long as the three of you wished to do that—and I might even sneak into some of your sessions, if you don't mind."

"Mind?" I asked. "God knows how welcome your presence would be, my friend."

The four of us went to the room Hafid had set aside for our scripture study, and I summarized the passages I had found in Jeremiah that pertained to either the Messiah or to the new covenant.

"Let me show you a few writings by Ezekiel that say essentially the same things," I added. "Ezekiel wrote that God would replace the people's hearts of stone with hearts of flesh, and would give them undivided hearts with a new spirit in them.[40] God also said this new covenant would be an everlasting one, and that he would make atonement for his people.[41] Do you have any questions about these scriptures?"

"Did either Jeremiah or Ezekiel say when God would make his new covenant?" Benjamin asked.

"I didn't see a precise date, but the implication of what I read is that this is part of what the Messiah was going to do," I said.

"Did you come across any other scriptures that talked about the Messiah?" Aaron asked.

"Possibly," I responded as I looked through the scroll of Ezekiel's writings. After a few minutes, I found the passage I was looking for, and read aloud some verses that said that God himself will be the good shepherd, though they also indicated that the good shepherd would be descended from David.[42]

"Wait a minute," Michael objected. "What you read says that God will place one shepherd over his people, and that the shepherd will be David, not a descendant of David."

"Yes, Michael, you are correct. But did David live before or after Ezekiel?"

"David lived hundreds of years before Ezekiel . . . Oh, I see," he exclaimed. "In other words, when the prophet says 'David' he is actually indicating that the good shepherd would be a descendant of David."

"Precisely."

---

[40] Ezekiel 11:19, 36:26-27.
[41] Ezekiel 16:60-63, 37:26.
[42] Ezekiel 34:11-24.

16.

I opened the scroll of Daniel's writings and began reading.

During the third year of King Jehoiakim's reign in Judah,
King Nebuchadnezzar of Babylon
Came to Jerusalem and besieged it.
The Lord gave him victory over King Jehoiakim of Judah...
Then King Nebuchadnezzar ordered his chief of staff
To bring to the palace some of the young men
Of Judah's royal family and other noble families,
Who had been brought to Babylon as captives.
"Select only strong, healthy, and good-looking young men," he said.
"Make sure they are well versed in every branch of learning,
Are gifted with knowledge and good judgment,
And are suited to serve in the royal palace.
Train these young men in the language and literature of Babylon."
They were to be trained for three years, and then they would
Enter the royal service. Daniel, Hananiah, Mishael, and Azariah
Were four of the young men chosen,
All from the tribe of Judah.
The chief of staff renamed them with these Babylonian names:
Daniel[43] was called Belteshazzar.[44]
Hananiah[45] was called Shadrach.[46]
Mishael[47] was called Meshach.[48] Azariah[49] was called Abednego.[50]

---

[43] Hebrew name meaning "God is my judge."
[44] Babylonian name meaning "Bel, protect his life!" Bel, also called Marduk, was the chief Babylonian god.
[45] Hebrew name meaning "YHWH shows grace."
[46] Babylonian name meaning "Under the command of Aku," the Babylonian moon god.
[47] Hebrew name meaning "Who is like God?"
[48] Babylonian name meaning "Who is like Aku?"
[49] Hebrew name meaning "YHWH helps."
[50] Babylonian name meaning "Servant of Nego," the Babylonian god of learning and writing. Daniel 1: 1-7.

"Why do you suppose the Babylonians changed the Jewish captives' names?" I asked.

When none of my friends answered, I explained what the Babylonian names meant.

"Oh," said Benjamin, nodding. "The Babylonians were apparently trying to switch the young men's religious allegiance from the one true God to their pagan deities."

"Very good," I replied. I then read the details about their training and diet, concluding with their surpassing all the other young men being trained for service to the king, which resulted in their being chosen to join the king's wise men and advisors.

While the four Jewish captives were still being trained for royal service, a crisis arose that almost resulted in their being killed along with the other wise men of Babylon. An extremely disturbing dream awoke King Nebuchadnezzar one night, and he was unable to go back to sleep. He called in his magicians, enchanters, sorcerers, and astrologers, and demanded that they tell him what he had dreamed and then interpret his dream for him.

> Then the astrologers answered the king, "Long live the king!
> Tell us the dream, and we will tell you what it means."
> But the king told the astrologers, "I am serious about this.
> If you don't tell me what my dream was
> And what it means, you will be torn apart
> And your houses will be turned into heaps of rubble!
> But if you tell me what I dreamed and what the dream means,
> I will give you many wonderful gifts and honors.
> Just tell me the dream and what it means."
> They said again, "Please, Your Majesty.
> Tell us the dream, and we will tell you its meaning."
> The king replied, "I know what you are doing!
> You're stalling for time because you know I'm serious when I say,

'If you don't tell me the dream, you are doomed.'
So you've conspired to tell me lies, hoping I'll change my mind.
Tell me the dream, and then I'll know you can tell me what it means."
The astrologers replied to the king,
"No one on earth can tell the king his dream!
And no king, however great and powerful,
Has ever asked such a thing of any magician,
Enchanter, or astrologer! The king's demand is impossible.
No one except the gods can tell you your dream,
And they do not live here among people."
The king was furious when he heard this,
And he ordered that all the wise men of Babylon be executed.
And because of the king's decree,
Men were sent to find and kill Daniel and his friends.
When Arioch, commander of the king's guard, came to kill them,
Daniel handled the situation with wisdom and discretion.
He asked Arioch, "Why has the king issued such a harsh decree?"
Arioch told him all that had happened.
Daniel went at once to see the king
And requested more time to tell the king what the dream meant.[51]

Daniel and his friends earnestly prayed to God, who revealed the secret to Daniel that night in a vision. After giving praises to the Lord, Daniel told Arioch not to kill the wise men, but to rather take him to the king. When the king asked Daniel if he could tell him the dream and reveal its meaning, Daniel humbly replied, "There are no wise men, enchanters, magicians, or fortune-tellers who can reveal the king's secret. But there is a God in heaven who reveals secrets, and he has shown King Nebuchadnezzar what will happen in the future. Now I will tell you your dream and the visions you saw as you lay on your bed."[52]

---

[51] Daniel 2: 4-16.

"In your vision, Your Majesty, you saw standing before you a huge,
shining statue of a man. It was a frightening sight.
The head of the statue was made of fine gold.
Its chest and arms were silver, its belly and thighs were bronze.
Its legs were iron,
And its feet were a combination of iron and baked clay.
As you watched, a rock was cut from a mountain,
But not by human hands.
It struck the feet of iron and clay, smashing them to bits.
The whole statue was crushed into small pieces
Of iron, clay, bronze, silver, and gold.
Then the wind blew them away without a trace,
Like chaff on a threshing floor.
But the rock that knocked the statue down
Became a great mountain that covered the whole earth.
That was the dream.
Now I will tell the king what it means.
Your Majesty, you are the greatest of kings.
The God of heaven has given you
Sovereignty, power, strength, and honor.
He has made you the ruler over all the inhabited world,
And has put even the wild animals and birds under your control.
You are the head of gold.
But after your kingdom comes to an end, another kingdom,
Inferior to yours, will rise to take your place.
After that kingdom has fallen, yet a third kingdom,
Represented by bronze, will rise to rule the world.
Following that kingdom, there will be a fourth one, as strong as iron.
That kingdom will smash and crush all previous empires,
Just as iron smashes and crushes everything it strikes.
The feet and toes you saw were a combination of iron and baked clay,

---

[52] Daniel 2: 27-28.

Showing that this kingdom will be divided.
Like iron mixed with clay, it will have some of the strength of iron.
But while some parts of it will be as strong as iron,
Other parts will be as weak as clay.
This mixture of iron and clay also shows that these kingdoms
Will try to strengthen themselves
By forming alliances with each other through intermarriage.
But they will not hold together, just as iron and clay do not mix.
During the reigns of those kings,
The God of heaven will set up a kingdom
That will never be destroyed or conquered.
It will crush all these kingdoms into nothingness,
And it will stand forever.
That is the meaning of the rock cut from the mountain,
Though not by human hands, that crushed to pieces
The statue of iron, bronze, clay, silver, and gold.
The great God was showing the king
What will happen in the future.
The dream is true, and its meaning is certain."[53]

I put the scroll down and looked at my friends.

"This is a remarkable prophesy," I said. "What are the four kingdoms?"

"Well, Daniel tells us the first one is Babylon under Nebuchadnezzar," Aaron answered.

"Good. What's next?"

"A kingdom represented by the silver portion of the statue," said Benjamin.

"And what kingdom took the place of Babylon?" I prompted.

"The Medes and Persians under Cyrus."

---

[53] Daniel 2: 31-45.

"Very good. What was the next great empire—the one represented by bronze?"

"I guess that would be the Greeks led by Alexander the Great," Aaron ventured.

"Excellent. What empire took the place of the Greeks and is as strong as iron, crushing everything it strikes?"

"The Roman Empire, of course."

"And what happens some time during the reign of the Roman Empire?" I asked.

"The God of heaven establishes his own kingdom," Aaron answered.

"That's what I failed to realize until it was forcefully driven home to me on the road to Damascus."

"Are you telling us that you think God has established his kingdom by allowing Jesus to be crucified?" Benjamin asked.

"I'm saying that the God of heaven has established his kingdom on Earth by sending the Messiah to be the perfect sacrifice for our sins."

"I thought the Messiah was supposed to establish an everlasting kingdom," Benjamin remarked.

"He has."

"But the Messiah is supposed to sit on David's throne and be an all-conquering leader."

"I think God's first priority was to redeem his people so that they could experience an everlasting fellowship with him. The all-conquering part comes later."

"When?"

"I don't know. Let's continue examining scripture and see what we can learn."

*****

Aaron and Michael joined me each day as we studied the scroll of Daniel's writings. Many of the events described were quite dramatic, such as Daniel's being thrown into the lions' den, his friends being placed into the blazing furnace, and the time the hand of God pronounced judgment on Babylon by writing "Mene, Mene, Tekel, Parsin" on the wall of the king's banquet hall.

Similarly, Daniel's visions were often strange and his prophesies were compelling. Since we were primarily looking for prophesies dealing with the Messiah, one especially stood out:

> A period of seventy sevens has been decreed for your people
> And your holy city to finish their rebellion,
> To put an end to their sin, to atone for their guilt,
> To bring in everlasting righteousness, to confirm the prophetic vision,
> And to anoint the Most Holy One. Now listen and understand!
> Seven sevens plus sixty-two sevens will pass from the time the command
> Is given to rebuild Jerusalem until the Anointed One comes.
> Jerusalem will be rebuilt with streets and strong defenses,
> Despite the perilous times.
> After sixty-two sevens, the Anointed One will be killed,
> Appearing to have accomplished nothing,
> And a ruler will arise whose armies will destroy the city and the temple.
> The end will come with a flood,
> And war and its miseries are decreed from that time to the very end.
> The ruler will make a treaty with the people for one seven,
> But after half this time, he will put an end to the sacrifices and offerings.
> And on the wing of abominations, he will set up a sacrilegious object
> That causes an abomination of desolation,
> Until the fate decreed for this defiler is finally poured out on him.[54]

We sat without speaking for several minutes. I looked at my two friends, who appeared to be as puzzled as I felt.

"What does that mean?" Aaron finally asked.

"I don't know," I admitted.

"Please," Michael pleaded. "Read it again."

After reading it a second time, I commented, "There seems to be three separate periods of time, though the first two periods appear to be connected. Seven sevens are in

---

[54] Daniel 9: 24-27.

the first period, sixty-two sevens in the second, and one seven in the third."

"How long is each seven?" Michael asked.

"Daniel doesn't say. It could be seven days, weeks, months, years, centuries, or some other period of time."

"Which unit is most likely?"

"Probably years," I answered. "But whatever it is, the commencement date is when the command was given to rebuild Jerusalem."

"Seven sevens would be forty-nine," mused Aaron. "What does that represent?"

I looked at Michael, but he only shrugged.

"Your guess may be as good as mine," I ventured, "but that is the approximate number of years it took to rebuild Jerusalem and the temple after the Babylonian captivity."

I got up from my chair and walked to a basket containing styluses and wax tablets enclosed in leather-covered wooden frames. Taking one of each, I returned to the table containing the scroll of Daniel's writings and began making some calculations. My friends watched me with rising curiosity.

"Yes!" I exclaimed victoriously a few minutes later. "I think it *is* years. Look at this! Daniel says seven sevens plus sixty-two sevens will pass from the time the command is given to rebuild Jerusalem until the Messiah—the Anointed One—comes and is killed. Seven times sixty-nine equals 483.

"Jesus died on the fourteenth day of Nisan in the year 3790,[55] which is almost exactly 483 years after the time the command was given to rebuild Jerusalem and the temple."[56]

"Really?" asked Michael.

---

[55] i.e., April 7, 30.

[56] Daniel would probably have been using a calendar with 360 days per year. 483 x 360 = 173,880 days, which misses the date Jesus was crucified by only a matter of a few months.

"Are you sure?" added Aaron.

"Yes, really—and here are my calculations."

Both men looked at my notes and mathematical calculations. I watched as their skepticism turned to wonder.

"That's incredible!" Aaron marveled.

"I agree," said Michael. "What about that last seven? Would it also be years?"

"If the first sixty-nine sevens represent 483 years, the last period would probably be a period of seven years," I said.

"When?" asked Michael.

"I don't know."

"Could it have already happened?"

"Possibly . . . well, I don't know. The temple was desecrated prior to Jesus' birth—and that led to the revolt led by the Maccabees," I mused. "But the rest of the prophesy doesn't fit. I suspect it is still unfulfilled and will happen sometime in the future."

"Well, just that part about the 483 years is remarkable enough for me!" said Aaron.

"Same here," Michael added.

"Is that enough to convince you that Jesus is the Messiah?" I asked.

"If it's not, it surely does come close to being the final nails needed to close the matter," Aaron muttered.

*****

The final nails were added as we studied the scrolls of the minor prophets over the next several weeks. Micah had written:

> But you, Bethlehem Ephrathah,
> Though you are small among the clans of Judah,
> Out of you will come for me one who will be the ruler over Israel,
> Whose origins are of old, from days of eternity.[57]

> He will stand and shepherd his flock in the strength of the LORD,
> In the majesty of the name of YHWH his God.
> And they will live securely,
> For then his greatness will reach to the ends of the earth.
> And he will be their peace.[58]

"You do know where Jesus was born, don't you?" I asked.

"No—but the way you asked the question causes me to strongly suspect that it was in Bethlehem Ephrathah," Michael answered.

Aaron nodded, smiled and said, "Yeah, I had heard that Jesus was born in Bethlehem, the city of David."

"If Jesus is the Son of God, his origins would definitely be old, from the days of eternity," I added.

"That's the part I still don't understand," Michael said. "How can Jesus be the Son of God? Wouldn't that mean there would be more than one God? Deuteronomy specifically says there is only one God."

"Remember that God is spirit," I said.

"So?"

"So . . . if God used a part of his own pure spirit to impregnate Jesus' mother, there will still be the same amount of God's spirit—still only one God—but now part of God would exist in human form."

"Why would God want to do that"

"Think, man. Think. God is eternal, right?"

"Right."

"That means he cannot die. Correct?"

"Correct."

"But a sacrificial animal must die in order to be a sacrifice."

---

[57] Micah 5:2.
[58] Micah 5:4-5a.

"True."

"By allowing part of himself to exist in human form, God could become the perfect sacrifice by dying on the cross for our sins."

"What do you mean by 'perfect sacrifice'?" Aaron asked.

"Every man and woman on earth has sinned. There is no way we can ever be good and righteous enough to earn our way to heaven. Only God can live a sinless life. By becoming a man known as Jesus, not only could God teach us and be an example for us, but he could also be tempted in all ways as we are but without sinning—thus allowing him to become the perfect sacrifice. Do you understand what I'm saying?"

"I think so. At least it's starting to make sense to me."

"That would also fulfill Isaiah's prophesies that the Messiah would be born of a virgin, would be called Immanuel,[59] would be pierced for our transgressions and crushed for our iniquities in order to become a guilt offering for our sins, and that by his stripes we are healed.

"It would explain how the Messiah could also be the mighty God and the Father of all eternity. It would also confirm Micah's words that the Messiah's origins are from ancient times, from the days of eternity. Indeed, he will shepherd his flock and will be their peace."

*****

We later read the words of Zechariah that prophesied:

Rejoice greatly, O Daughter of Zion!
Shout, Daughter of Jerusalem!
See, your king comes to you, righteous and having salvation,
Gentle and riding on a donkey, on a colt, the foal of a donkey.
I will take away the chariots from Ephraim

---

[59] Which means "God with us."

> And the war-horses from Jerusalem,
> And the battle bow will be broken.
> He will proclaim peace to the nations.
> His rule will extend from sea to sea
> And from the River to the ends of the earth.[60]

"If you will recall," I said, "Jesus rode triumphantly into Jerusalem on a colt, the foal of a donkey, the Sunday before he was crucified."

"He did," Aaron acknowledged. "But that is less impressive to me, since he could merely be deliberately doing it in order to fulfill Zechariah's prophesy."

"True," I conceded. "Nevertheless, even that prophesy was fulfilled. It remains to be seen whether his message spreads from sea to sea and to the ends of the earth."

We were unable to come to a clear consensus among ourselves about whether Zechariah's notation that God's cornerstone would come from Judah[61] was a reference to the Messiah, but we did agree that the prophet was apparently talking about the Messiah when he wrote:

> I will pour out on the house of David
> And the inhabitants of Jerusalem
> A spirit of grace and supplication.
> They will look on me, the one they have pierced,
> And they will mourn for him as one mourns for an only child,
> And grieve bitterly for him as one grieves for a firstborn son.
> On that day the weeping in Jerusalem will be great.[62]

"Jesus is the one they pierced, they looked on him, and many grieved for him," I said. "However, I am not sure whether this passage is referring to his crucifixion, death

---

[60] Zechariah 9: 9-10.
[61] Zechariah 10: 4.
[62] Zechariah 12: 10-11.

and burial, or whether it is discussing a time yet to come. What do you think?"

My friends were also unable to determine the timeline Zechariah's vision foretold. However, we were much more certain of the prophet's other Messianic prophesies:

> "Awake, O sword, against my shepherd,
> Against the man who is close to me!"
> Declares the LORD Almighty.
> "Strike the shepherd, and the sheep will be scattered."[63]

"That reminds me of what I have been told happened in the Garden of Gethsemane when the soldiers sent by the high priest arrested Jesus," Aaron remarked.

"Yes," I replied. "All of Jesus' disciples scattered and fled when the soldiers struck Jesus and arrested him."

---

[63] Zechariah 13: 7.

17.

"Good morning, Saul. Do you mind if I visit with you for a few minutes?"

I looked up to see Hafid standing outside my bedroom. "Of course not," I replied with a smile. "I appreciate your hospitality and kindness. Please, have a seat," and I gestured toward a chair.

Hafid sat down, leaned forward and said, "An old friend of mine from Jerusalem stopped by to see me earlier today, and I thought you might be interested in meeting him."

I looked at Hafid questioningly, and he continued, "Joseph of Arimathea is the owner of many caravans. Since I have been a rather successful salesman, it is perhaps only natural that we would get to know each other . . . and become friends.

"I know that you have become a follower of Jesus. You might possibly be interested in meeting Joseph, since he was the man who buried Jesus after the crucifixion. He is also a believer and follower of the Christ."

"By all means!" I exclaimed as I got up from my chair.

We walked to a covered courtyard that opened onto a private garden.

"Saul, I'd like you to meet Joseph of Arimathea," Hafid said, gesturing to a man who walked forward to greet me. "Joseph, this is Saul of Tarsus, who is currently staying with me."

"We have met before," Joseph remarked. "We are both members of the Sanhedrin, though I haven't seen Saul there for a while. Been rather busy, I understand."

Hafid motioned for us to recline on couches that formed two sides of a triangle. Hafid took his place on the third couch, while Erasmus brought bowls of fruit for us to eat while reclining and visiting.

"I told Joseph about your experience on the road here," Hafid said.

"It sounds as if you have met Jesus even more recently than my encounters with him," Joseph remarked.

"That's true. You are familiar with how Jesus changed my life. I am anxious to hear about how he changed yours."

"Didn't you go down to the Jordan River with the Sanhedrin delegation to see John the Baptist back when he was beginning to baptize people?" Joseph asked me.

"Yes. I was invited by my old teacher, Gamaliel."

"Do you remember how John told the crowd that he was preparing the way for the coming Messiah?"

"Yes. I remember."

"Well, I decided that with all my caravans and other business interests, it was important for me to be kept fully informed about anything as momentous as the Messiah."

"What did you do?"

"I assigned my best investigator to watch John and to notify me whenever the person John spoke about appeared. After John baptized Jesus, I assigned a second investigator to the case."

"What did you learn?"

"Enough to decide that Jesus was indeed the promised Messiah. But then he threw me for a loop by getting crucified."

"Why did that . . . ?" I started to ask.

"Well, I had always understood that the Messiah would reign forever. He can't very well do that if he's dead, can he? To me, Jesus' crucifixion effectively showed he was not the Messiah."

"So why did you take him down from the cross and bury him?"

Joseph lightly laughed. "Partly because of what I had learned in my investigations, and partly because of something that happened almost three years before Jesus was crucified.

"My closest friend is Nicodemus, another Pharisee and member of the Sanhedrin. The night after the first time Jesus cleansed the temple by overturning the tables of the money changers and sellers of livestock, Nicodemus and I met with him. At the end of that meeting, Jesus laid his hands on the two of us and prayed that we would have the courage to do what was right.

"As I stood on the hill of execution known as Golgotha, it suddenly became clear to me that it would not be right for Jesus not to have a proper Jewish burial." Joseph chuckled as he added, "I believe Nicodemus thought I was crazy . . . and he may have been right."

"Why do you say that?"

"Think about it. Throughout the time I was being fed information by my investigators, I was slowly coming to the conclusion that Jesus is the Messiah—but I never took a stand for him, never identified with him, and never professed any belief in him. Now when everything appeared lost and his impending death seemed to snuff out any hope of his being the Messiah, I was ready to finally take a stand. If that's not craziness, what is?

"Plus, touching a dead body would make me ceremonially unclean for seven full days—which would mean I couldn't take part in the Passover Sabbath. Placing Jesus' body in the tomb that had been prepared for my family meant none of us could ever use it, since a convicted criminal's body had defiled it."

"Then why did you do it?"

"During my investigations, I had come to have the highest regard for Jesus and his teachings. I was convinced that giving him a proper burial and placing him in my own tomb was the right and proper thing to do."

"What did that entail?"

"I first went to my Jerusalem shipping office and got some of my men to come with me to help. Then we returned to Golgotha and watched while Jesus died. As soon as the Romans had confirmed that he was dead, I went to Governor Pilate and asked for the body. He sent one of his subordinates to accompany me and to tell the centurion to release Jesus' body to me after confirming he was dead.

"The Roman soldiers removed Jesus from the cross, and my men transported him to the new tomb that had been prepared for my family and me. We washed Jesus' body and massaged his arms, which had hardened in an outstretched position. After Jesus had been washed according to Jewish burial customs, we wrapped the body in long linen cloth. Nicodemus had brought about a hundred libra[64] of myrrh, aloe and similar burial spices, and we put those in the folds of the linen cloth to help offset the stench of the decomposing body. We tied a separate napkin under Jesus' chin to keep his mouth from opening as the muscles loosened. Finally, we rolled the large disk-shaped stone along its curved path to firmly block the entrance to the tomb."

"Is it true that guards were posted around the tomb?"

"Yes, that's true. In fact, both Roman soldiers and temple guards were posted . . . Oh! . . . That reminds me!" Joseph exclaimed as he got up from his couch and walked over to a small travel bag he had apparently brought with him. Opening the bag, he took out a long seamless reddish brown cloak, which he handed to Hafid.

"What's this?" Hafid asked.

---

[64] i.e., about seventy-five pounds

"See if you recognize it," Joseph replied.

Hafid carefully inspected the garment, feeling its texture and noting the amount of wear and tear it had received over the years. The old man suddenly reversed the robe and examined an area along the hem. His face broke into a broad smile as he murmured, "Ah, yes . . . the star of Tola—together with the mark of Pathros. My master and mentor used to sell these *abeyah* robes."

"You once told me this was the type of robe that led to your great success," Joseph prodded.

"True . . . true," the old man nodded. "Where did you get this particular robe?"

"This is the robe worn by Jesus when he was being prepared for crucifixion. The Roman soldiers divided his other garments among themselves. Since this robe was seamless and was worth as much as all the rest combined, they cast lots for it. I purchased it from the winner. When I saw the markings inside the robe, I realized it might be similar to the one you had earlier mentioned to me . . . so I brought it to you."

"Thank you, my friend. Please tell me whatever you know about the birth of this Jesus."

"Jesus left our world with few worldly possessions. He entered it with even less. He was born in a cave, in Bethlehem, during the time of the census of Augustus."

Hafid's eyes clouded with tears, which he brushed away with his hand as he softly asked, "And was there not the brightest star that man has ever seen which shone above the birthplace of this baby?"

Joseph thought for a moment before answering. "Yes, there was a bright star that guided the wise men as they journeyed to Bethlehem, where they presented gifts of gold, frankincense and myrrh."

"Thank you, Joseph. This robe means more to me than you can guess."

"Excuse me," I interjected. "Would you mind telling me more about those wise men and their gifts?"

"I gave my top investigator—a fellow named Joshua—the assignment of interviewing Jesus' mother, Mary. She told Joshua that one evening when Jesus was just a toddler they were startled by a procession of camels bearing a group of grandly dressed men who claimed to be wise men from the East who were looking for the new king of the Jews. When they saw Jesus, they all bowed down and worshiped him. Then they gave Mary and Joseph expensive gifts of gold, frankincense, and myrrh."

"Gold, frankincense, and myrrh," I repeated. "How unusual, but yet . . . how appropriate!"

Joseph and Hafid looked at me with rather blank but questioning faces. "Think about it," I challenged. "Those are not the typical gifts for a new baby or even a young child. Nevertheless, they are extremely appropriate for this particular child."

Their quizzical gaze invited me to continue.

"Gold is a wonderful gift for anyone, any time—but especially for royalty such as the King of Kings. Frankincense is incense that is burned in temples to offer a bittersweet perfume for the gods. Why not use it to honor Heaven's deity, the Lord of Lords? And we have already discussed how myrrh is used in burials to offset the smell of decaying bodies. It's an incredibly unusual gift for a baby—but most appropriate for the one who would be the perfect sacrifice for our sins."

Joseph nodded, smiled and said, "My, my, Saul . . . How you have changed since the last time I saw you. In and around Jerusalem, you were practically breathing fire against the followers of Jesus. Each time one of them was brought up before the Sanhedrin, you led the charge to find him guilty—if I am remembering events correctly."

"Unfortunately, your memory is correct," I admitted. "All my life I had been taught that there is only one true God who created all else that exists. 'Hear, O Israel: The Lord our God, the Lord is one.'[65] I firmly believed that it was blasphemy for anyone to claim that God had a Son named Jesus. Wouldn't that be two separate deities—two Gods instead of only one?"

"I had precisely that same problem," Joseph mused, "but three things helped clear it up for me."

"What three things?"

"When Joshua—that's my investigator, remember?—was interviewing Mary, she told him that she had been visited by the angel Gabriel prior to becoming pregnant with Jesus. Gabriel told her she was going to give birth to a son whom she was to name Jesus because he would save his people from their sins. Mary asked Gabriel how she could give birth to a son, since she was a virgin. Gabriel responded that the Lord God Almighty—*Yahweh Elohim*—would use a part of his own pure spirit to impregnate Mary so that the child born to her would be the Son of God.

"The second thing that helped clear it up for me was my good friend Nicodemus, who pointed out several scriptures that helped him. He reminded me that God is a spirit who can be or appear however he chooses."

"Yes!" I exclaimed. "I remember that from Gamaliel's teachings. In fact, one of the meanings for the name God chose for himself—*Yahweh*—is 'I AM who I choose to be.'"[66]

"Precisely!" Joseph said emphatically. "You made the point I was about to make. If God chooses to use part of his spirit to become a man, there is still the same amount of pure divine spirit—still one God—but now part is in human form, subject to human limitations, and able to die as the perfect sacrifice for our sins.

---

[65] Deuteronomy 6: 4.
[66] Exodus 3:14.

"Nicodemus also pointed out a scripture in Isaiah where that great prophet referred to the coming Messiah as both the mighty God and as the everlasting Father."[67]

"Really? That's the scripture Nicodemus used for showing that Jesus is both the Son of God and the promised Messiah?"

"Yes . . ." Joseph seemed mystified by my outburst.

"Sorry for the interruption. I was just startled because that's the same scripture I read in the Damascus synagogue the first Sabbath after my encounter with Jesus on the road here . . . when he converted me. I told the people about how Jesus had appeared to me and asked why I was persecuting him, and I used that very same scripture to show how the greatest of our Jewish prophets had used those terms for the promised Messiah—terms that would normally be considered blasphemous—but it wasn't blasphemy because it was God himself who was doing it."

"You said all that in the Damascus synagogue?"

"Yes."

"And you used that particular scripture?"

"The scroll on the *bimah* was opened to that passage."

"That's precisely the same point Nicodemus made to me[68] prior to Jesus' death, burial and resurrection."

"You said there were three things that helped clear it up for you. What's the third?"

"I had my own encounters with Jesus after the resurrection. A few hours after he rose from the grave, Jesus appeared to Cleopas and me on the road to Emmaus and explained the scriptures that prophesied about him. Then later that evening Jesus appeared to his disciples. Cleopas and I were still there with the disciples at the time because we had been telling them about our earlier encounter with the risen Christ. Jesus opened all our minds

---

[67] Isaiah 9:6.
[68] *Nicodemus' Quest*, p. 89.

so that we were no longer confused about the meanings of the scriptures."

"Thank you so much for sharing that with me," I said.

"It was my pleasure to do so, Saul. I am thrilled to learn of your conversion. What are your plans now?"

"I am currently going through an in-depth study of the scriptures with a couple of my friends from Cilicia."

"You already have an outstanding education as a result of being taught by Gamaliel. What are you trying to learn?"

"Yes, I was taught well by Gamaliel—but . . . well, quite frankly . . . I want to know how I managed to go so wrong in my application of the Scriptures. As you noted a few minutes ago, I was practically breathing fire as I sought to wipe out this dangerous new cult of people who think Jesus is the Son of God."

"At least you were pursuing your goals with drive, intensity, and conviction."

"Yes . . . unfortunately . . . there certainly was conviction. In fact, there were more convictions than I now want to admit, though I once took pride in them. I helped convict many fine, noble people who apparently knew the truth about Jesus—and were punished for it. They and their families remain continually in my prayers. I must atone for the wrongs I have committed. I need to direct my drive, intensity, and . . . conviction . . . toward spreading the good news about Jesus."

"You now embrace the gospel you fought—and call it good news?"

"Most definitely. The news that God loves us enough to enter our world to redeem us and give us everlasting life with him has to be the best news of all time! I just thank God that Jesus was also willing to intervene in my life by appearing to me on the road to Damascus, stopping me in my tracks and redirecting my life."

"You have definitely changed since the time you left Jerusalem." Joseph turned toward Hafid and said, "Thank you, old friend, for bringing me up to date on the transformation that has occurred in Brother Saul."

"Brother?"

"Yes, Saul is now my brother in Christ."

Hafid held up the robe and said to Joseph, "And thank you, my friend, for this miraculous robe."

"Miraculous?" asked Joseph.

"Yes, Joseph. I am reasonably sure that this is not merely *like* the robe that opened the door to my success as a salesman. Rather, I think that it *is* that robe."

Hafid turned to me and said, "Since Joseph knows the story, I won't take the time now to tell it again. However, I will share it with you later when we are alone together."

"I will look forward to it," I responded.

18.

When we visited privately the next day, Hafid told me how Jesus' robe helped him rise from being a humble camel boy to become an extremely rich and well-respected salesman. He also introduced me to a set of scrolls that he said were the secret of his success.[69]

"If you learn and internalize the contents of these scrolls and diligently follow their instructions, there is no reason you can't have the same type of success," Hafid promised. "Indeed, I firmly believe you will become an even greater and more successful salesman than I have been."

"But I am not interested in selling products," I answered. "Rather, I am driven to tell others the good news about Jesus Christ."

"What is that but salesmanship?" Hafid asked. "My product was merchandise; yours may be salvation and eternal life—but both involve spreading the good news about the product we wish to 'sell' to our audience."

I thought about what he said—and realized Hafid was right. "When should I start?"

"You may start immediately, if you wish . . . but I would prefer for you to keep this education process quiet and not mention it to the others, at least for the time being."

I agreed to do as Hafid suggested. I spent the next year reading, rereading, memorizing, and internalizing each scroll

---

[69] Read the story in Og Mandino's book *The Greatest Salesman in the World.*

as dictated by the contents of the scrolls. Hafid and I also spent a considerable amount of time in private discussions and prayer, though we sometimes also included Hafid's trusted servant, Erasmus.

*****

One day as I was looking over my notes, I heard a knock at my door. "Who is it?" I asked.

"Sorry to disturb you," answered Erasmus, "but there is a man here who wants to see you. He said to tell you his name is Barnabas."

"Barnabas?" I responded, mystified. "I don't think I know any Barnabas."

"He said you wouldn't know him by that name—but he also said he would be most surprised if you didn't remember him once you actually saw him."

"Congratulations, Erasmus. You've succeeded in arousing my curiosity," I said as I got up from my work and went with him to the covered courtyard where I had previously met with Hafid and Joseph of Arimathea. This man was considerably younger than those men, but he was definitely familiar to me.

"Joseph!" I exclaimed with surprise when I saw him. "I certainly didn't expect to see one of my fellow disciples of Gamaliel! How did you find me here?"

"Joseph of Arimathea told me you were staying with Hafid in Damascus . . . and that you have become a believer in Jesus Christ. Is that true?"

"Yes, it is most assuredly true. Did he also tell you about my encounter with Jesus on the road here?"

"He did, and he seemed most impressed with you. Of course, that part didn't surprise me, since you were Gamaliel's prize student."

"Watch it, Joseph. Flattery will get you . . . almost anywhere. But you have aroused my curiousity."

"About what?"

"About the name you're using. Gamaliel and his disciples always called you Joseph."

"That's right."

"If your name is Joseph, why did you ask Erasmus to say that someone called Barnabas wanted to see me?"

"Barnabas is the nickname I have been given by others in the church."

"Why?"

"I'm not entirely sure. They claim it's because I'm always encouraging everyone and being such a positive influence—I think Barnabas means *son of encouragement* in Hebrew—but I suspect it may really be because there are just simply too many Josephs in the Jerusalem church. Being called Barnabas helps me stand out from the rest of the crowd of Josephs."

"You must also be a follower of Jesus."

"That I am, Saul—and glad of it."

Joseph—or Barnabas—stayed with Hafid for several days. I told him additional details about my conversion and other events that had happened. He was sorry to hear about Jonathan but was very encouraged about virtually everything else.

"Are you ready to get back to work?" he eventually asked me.

"What do you mean?"

"Jesus appeared to you for a reason—and I strongly suspect it was more than just to halt your destruction of his church."

Again I asked, "What do you mean?"

"You were probably the most organized, logical thinker among all of Gamaliel's students and disciples, and you were the most forceful and persuasive debater I have ever known. I think God wants to make use of your considerable talents. Are you ready to put those talents to good use? Are you ready to go to work—this time for your Lord and Savior, whom you previously opposed?"

"Wat are you proposing?"

"Tomorrow is the Sabbath. Why don't we go to at least one of the synagogues in Damascus and begin telling the people the good news you've discovered?"

19.

"Saul! It's good to see you back in the synagogue again," Rabbi Benjamin commented to me the next day.

"It's good to be back in the Lord's house, my friend. Rabbi Benjamin, I'd like you to meet an old friend of mine; this is Jos . . . er . . . Barnabas."

"I'm pleased to meet you. I'm not certain I correctly caught your name. Is it Jozer Barnabas?"

"No. Not quite. Saul knew me as Joseph, which is my given name. However, the last several years I have been primarily going by Barnabas, the nickname given to me by my friends in Jerusalem. I fear that Saul may be having trouble adjusting to the new name."

"Barnabas and I were both disciples of Gamaliel in Jerusalem," I said.

"Are you also a member of the Sanhedrin?" Benjamin asked Barnabas.

"No. I cannot say that I've had that honor."

"Well, welcome to Damascus—and to our humble synagogue."

"Thank you, Rabbi Benjamin. *Shalom.*"

"*Shalom.*"

"Come," I said as I lightly touched Barnabas' left arm. "I want to introduce you to some other friends." I led him toward a couple that had just walked into the room. "This is Ananias and his wife, Rachel. The Lord sent Ananias to restore my sight after I had been blinded on the road to Damascus." Turning to them, I added, "And this is Barnabas, a fellow believer from Jerusalem."

After they had greeted each other, I quietly asked Ananias, "Have you had any more trouble since returning to your home here in Damascus?"

"No. We've been back about a year, and haven't been bothered. When we first moved out, we asked some trusted neighbors to keep watch on our house for us."

"Did they observe anything suspicious?"

"The ruffians who were trying to catch you apparently laid in ambush near our house for awhile, and they continued to watch it for several weeks before eventually giving up. Our neighbors reported seeing men they didn't recognize occasionally hanging around the neighborhood off and on for several months."

"It sounds as if it was a good thing we all left when we did."

"I agree."

"I'm sorry your kindness and hospitality toward me caused you so much trouble."

"Think nothing of it, Saul. Rachel and I are glad we were able to play a tiny part in the Lord's plans for you. Besides, we had wanted to visit Rachel's parents in Caesarea for quite some time; this gave us a great excuse . . . plus, we were able to witness to them as well. Now they are also believers in Jesus."

"That's wonderful!" I exclaimed.

"It's truly an answer to our prayers, isn't it?" Ananias asked, glancing at Rachel.

Her broad smile easily answered his question. Then she turned her radiant face toward me and said, "Thank you for helping to make it possible."

"Me?" I asked. "What did I do?"

"First you came into our home as a most unwelcome guest . . . to my way of thinking, at least . . . and showed me I needed to trust in the Lord's provisions and guidance—not to mention his ability to change and transform lives.

"Next, you broadened my outlook and deepened my faith with your knowledge of scriptures and how they applied to Jesus. Finally, the imminent threat posed by those who sought to arrest you caused us to go to my parents, which resulted in their conversion."

Again, her smile was dazzling—and appeared genuine. It was almost amazing how her countenance had changed from the first time we met. Was this the same terrified woman who had cowered at the sight of me? I breathed a quick silent prayer of gratitude for the transformation.

Rabbi Benjamin called upon Barnabas to come forward to the *bimah*, where the scroll of Isaiah's prophesies had been opened to the passage about how God's suffering servant would be despised, rejected, tortured and killed.[70] Barnabas' voice cracked and almost broke as he read about how the unnamed man was pierced for our transgressions, was crushed for our iniquities, and was buried in a rich man's grave, but it reverberated as he read the part about how his punishment brings peace for us.

Looking up from the scroll, Barnabas said, "We Jews have for centuries looked forward to the coming Messiah. We like to picture him as an all-conquering warrior who will sit on the throne of his ancestor David and will rule forever. We often overlook or even purposely ignore passages such as the one I have read to you today, which remind us that the Messiah's purpose and mission is more than merely being a king or ruler. He is God's great gift to a spiritually impoverished world that is dying in its sins.

"As the Scripture says, all we like sheep have gone astray.[71] Just as sheep may not intend to wander away from a shepherd's protection, we may not have deliberately wandered away from God. Nevertheless, there are times we all have gone astray. We have all sinned and fallen short of

---

[70] Isaiah 53.
[71] Isaiah 53:6.

God's glory—but God reached out and extended his glory to us.

"I'm here to tell you the good news that the ancient prophecies have been fulfilled, and the new covenant has been inaugurated by the coming of the Messiah. He was born of King David's family and lineage, he lived and ministered to us as had been prophesied, and then he suffered and died as foretold in the scriptures I have just read to you in order to redeem us and save us from our sins.

"As Isaiah prophesied, the Messiah was pierced for our transgressions and was crushed for our iniquities. The punishment that brought us peace was upon him, and by his wounds we are healed.[72] He was buried in a rich man's grave, rose again on the third day as prophesied, met with hundreds of people—most of whom are still alive—after his death and resurrection, and is now exalted at God's right hand as the Son of God, the Lord of Lords, and the Savior of all who place their trust and belief in him.

"I can personally attest that he has given his Holy Spirit to his followers as an assurance of his Lordship and as a foretaste of both the glory we will have in heaven and of his future return, when he will fulfill the remaining prophesies about him."

Barnabas' eyes swept over the assembled people in the synagogue as he momentarily paused. Then he continued, "The prophesies were true, the Messiah has come, and God's grace is real. The new and better covenant promised by Jeremiah[73] has been implemented, and it has changed my life. I have a joy I cannot describe that is beyond anything I could have imagined while I was trying to live by the letter of the law and trusting that to somehow save me. Now that I've experienced God's forgiveness, grace,

---

[72] Isaiah 53:5.
[73] Jeremiah 31:31-35.

justification, and cleansing power, I have a joy that fills my soul and makes life so much more wonderful."

Barnabas stood silently beside the *bimah* for a few moments as if he wanted to say more but thought better of it. Instead, he nodded to Benjamin and then returned to where he had been sitting before being asked by the rabbi to read from the scroll.

After the service ended, over a dozen Jews crowded around Barnabas and me. A few were those who had previously accepted Jesus as their Lord and Savior, and who now welcomed both Barnabas and his comments. Several others angrily denounced Barnabas as being a dangerous radical who committed blasphemy by referring to the Messiah as being the Son of God.

A much larger group did not crowd around us. Rather, they hung back listening to the comments made by the others—and to our responses. By and large, these were people who were seeking . . . something.

Some of them were seeking information; they had questions that needed answers, or were simply curious. Many had heard gossip or rumors, and all had heard Barnabas' comments.

Some were seeking the joy and satisfaction Barnabas claimed to have found, and they wanted to know more.

Some were seeking God. That may have been why they were in the synagogue in the first place. They needed to establish a personal link with the One who had created the universe, and had not found that personal relationship in Judaism or in keeping the Law of Moses.

Some were seeking to fill a spiritual void in their lives. Financial success, fame and fortune, worldly pleasures, and even interpersonal relationships had only satisfied them up to a point. They sensed that something was missing. It was as if their Creator had made them with a void that only he could fill—but they were at a loss as to how that could be done.

Some sought to answer personal problems that weighed on their minds and spirits. Some were discouraged, downtrodden and hopeless, while others found that hope had been rekindled by Barnabas' words. Some recognized themselves in Isaiah's description of the sheep that had gone astray . . . and they desperately wanted to find their way home to the Good Shepherd.

Barnabas and I visited with all of them who wished to talk with us. After we had visited in the synagogue for awhile, we gradually worked our way outside and sat under the shade of some trees. Ananias, Rachel and several other believers also remained behind to visit with the seekers. Finally Ananias told the rest of us, "I've thoroughly enjoyed meeting with all of you, but we probably would be more comfortable at our house. Any of you who would like to continue visiting are most welcome to come with us."

Fourteen of us went with Ananias and Rachel to their home. About half of us were believers. The others were seekers who wished to visit further. Four of the seekers accepted Christ as their savior and joined other followers of Christ the next day when we met for a Lord's Day worship service in the home of a believer named Mark.

Over the next several weeks I continued to visit with various people who were seeking answers. Some I had met at the synagogues, while others were their friends and relatives. I visited in various homes, businesses, and public parks and marketplaces in and around Damascus. Sometimes I debated with Jews or Gentiles who angrily denounced my beliefs, but most of the time I simply proclaimed the truth I had learned about Jesus Christ.

Barnabas stayed with me for one additional Sabbath and Lord's Day before heading back to Jerusalem. As we parted, I promised I would come to visit him in Jerusalem. I had no idea how soon that would turn out to be.

20.

Late one afternoon a few weeks later, I was walking north on the Cardo Maximus heading toward the Northern Gate of Damascus when I first became aware of the soldiers. I'm still not sure what caused me to notice them, but some sixth sense alerted me that their actions seemed a bit suspicious.

I continued walking north for about half a block until I came to an open market. Turning into the market, I walked briskly down the line of stalls where vendors peddled their goods. When I got about three-quarters of the way through the market, I stopped at one of the stalls, ostensibly to examine a trinket—but I was really using the action as an opportunity to glance back toward the entrance. Two soldiers had entered the market and appeared to be looking around.

I darted in between two of the stalls and slipped out a side entrance. As I did so, I heard a yell from a third soldier who had been crossing the street toward the front of the market when he caught sight of me.

Ducking behind a mud brick fence, I ran until I came to a space between two houses, and then ran through that opening toward another street. As I approached the street, I saw a wagon containing a load of hay. I jumped onto the wagon, wrapped my head cloth around my face, and worked my way under the straw.

As I attempted to lie as quietly as I could, I heard the sound of running feet and heavy breathing. Someone had stopped in the street adjacent to the wagon. Within moments he was joined by at least two other persons who had apparently also been running and who were now attempting to catch their breath. Although my heartbeat quickened, my breathing slowed and became as shallow as possible.

"Where'd he go?" one of the men asked the others.

"I followed him through the space between those two houses but didn't see which direction he took on this street."

"He can't be very far ahead of us, but we can't waste time talking. You two go that way, and we'll take this direction. Check any side street or object he can hide behind. Capture him if you can—but kill him if you must. Move out!"

So they are chasing me, and are prepared to kill me! But why? As far as I knew, I had broken no law and had done nothing wrong. Yet someone had given these soldiers orders to arrest me or even kill me. What person in authority had I offended to that extent? I couldn't think of anyone.

But a more immediate problem forced its way into my consciousness. *What should I do now? Where could I go?*

Someone with the power to command soldiers had ordered that I be captured or killed. Was there anyone I could trust who had sufficient power or authority to give me shelter and protection in the face of such an order?

I can trust the other believers—but do any of them have sufficient power to resist the authority of whoever is ordering these soldiers? I thought and prayed for several minutes. As I did so, the mental picture of Hafid crystallized in my mind. Yes, he was both a believer and was influential enough. But his estate was well outside the walls of Damascus. Could I safely make it through the city gates, or were they being watched? I knew I had to find out the answer.

I cautiously raised my head through the hay and looked around. There were no soldiers in sight. I mentally mapped out a route that gave me maximum cover while leading me where I wished to go. Since it was almost dusk, I thought about staying under the hay and waiting until it was dark before making my move. Then I remembered that the gates to the city were often closed at sundown. I needed to get to the gates—and I didn't have much time.

Since the soldiers had observed me heading for Damascus' Northern Gate, I decided it would probably be safer for me to attempt to exit through the Western Gate of the city. Rather than using Straight Street for the approach, I slipped down various back streets, alleys and spaces between buildings until I finally got to a concealed spot under a bush next to a stone fence, from which I could observe the gate without being seen.

There were the usual contingents of soldiers patrolling the city wall, plus the unseen ones inside the guard towers. Were any of them specifically looking for me, I wondered.

I received my answer after a few minutes of watching when a farmer's cart attempted to leave the city. Four soldiers came out of the shadows, intercepted the cart, and made the driver dismount. One soldier guarded the driver, one held the reins to the farmer's horse, and a third soldier inspected the cart. The fourth soldier guarded the roadway so that no one else could pass while the cart was being examined. *They're looking for something or someone, all right. Probably me.*

If I can't make it to Hafid's house outside the city, can I get to one of his properties inside Damascus? Benjamin had once told me Hafid owned various places in the city. *How can I find out if Hafid has a place that might work for me?* Even as I mentally formulated the question, I knew the answer.

Again I made a mental map of where I needed to go before slipping out from my hiding place . . . and again I used various back streets, alleys and spaces between buildings to get there. Several times soldiers crossed my path, and I had to freeze and melt into the shadows.

Eventually I made it to my destination and lightly knocked on a familiar door.

"Saul?" queried a surprised Benjamin when he opened the door.

"Shhh," I warned. "Are you alone?"

"Yes. Come in."

"Thank you," I said, slipping gratefully into the rabbi's house.

"What brings you here at this hour?"

"Do you know anything about an order being issued for my arrest?"

"Only the one you told me about a few years ago. Why?"

"Several soldiers chased me this afternoon. I overheard one of them tell the others to capture me if they could, but also giving them clearance to kill me if they needed to."

"Were they city soldiers or Roman soldiers?"

"Their uniforms were similar to those worn by Roman soldiers, but I'm not sure whether they actually were Roman uniforms; I guess I don't know who they are. I do know they appear to be watching the city gates and are examining anyone who attempts to leave town."

"That will make it difficult to get word to Hafid. That is where you have been staying, isn't it?"

"Yes."

Benjamin thought for a few minutes. Then he said, "You may stay here tonight if you wish. I have an extra mat you may use. What else do you need from me?"

"I need a safe place where I can hide until I can get out of town. You once told me Hafid owned properties all over Damascus. I was hoping one of them might suffice. Also, I'd like to find out who issued the order for my capture or death."

"I'll try to get in touch with Hafid and see what I can find out tomorrow. Meanwhile, you are welcome to stay here."
"Thank you."
"You are most welcome, my friend."

21.

Benjamin left his house early the next morning and did not return until the middle of the afternoon.

"I sent a message to Hafid this morning, and he responded by sending Erasmus into Damascus to inspect his properties and to choose which one will best serve your needs. You are to meet Erasmus at the location indicated on this map."

Benjamin handed me a crudely drawn sketch.

"Can you find your way from here to that house?" he asked.

"I think so."

"Good. Since I suspect yesterday's soldiers will have given others a description of what you were wearing yesterday, it would probably be prudent to change your clothing."

"This is all I have at the moment."

"I understand, but I have some other garments you can change into . . . or put on over what you have on now."

Benjamin handed me a cloak and headdress that appeared identical to what he was wearing. He smiled and said, "Now you can be me as you go from this place . . . in case anyone is watching this house."

"Did you see anyone?"

"No—and I was looking. But it doesn't hurt to be careful."

I nodded and said, "I agree."

A few minutes later I walked out of Benjamin's house dressed in his spare clothes, and attempted to mimic the rabbi's walk and gait as I strolled toward the address he had indicated on his map.

Twice I encountered soldiers, but neither group appeared to notice me. The first contingent was busy talking among themselves, while the second group appeared to be searching for something . . . or someone—but I was able to pass by without incident.

When I arrived at the address, I knocked lightly on the door.

No one answered.

I knocked again.

Still no answer.

I pushed open the door and glanced inside. "Is anyone here?" I asked.

Silence. I walked in and looked around.

The small house consisted of three rooms. A few chairs, tables and mats were scattered around, but I saw no one. I sat down in a chair and waited.

After about an hour, I heard a light knock at the front door, followed by momentary silence. Then the door opened and Erasmus walked in.

"Greetings," he said.

"Hello, Erasmus."

He placed a bag on a table, looked up at me, and said, "I've got several salted fish and loaves of bread for you to eat. You can stay here until we find a safe way to get you out of town."

"As far as I know, I've broken no laws. Why are the soldiers seeking to arrest or kill me?"

"According to Hafid's sources, the Jewish religious leaders want to silence you, and have bribed the governor under King Aretas[74] to either arrest you or kill you. The order has been passed on to a local centurion."

---

[74] Aretas IV was king of Arabia/Nabataea, which included Damascus.

"I guess that shows how much protection one gets from being a Roman citizen!"

"Er . . . sorry," Erasmus stammered, "but I'm not following what you're saying."

"I would have thought a centurion—or a governor, for that matter—would have been more hesitant to order a death sentence for a Roman citizen who has not committed a crime—especially without a trial."

"Do you mean . . . Are you a Roman citizen, Saul?"

"I am."

"I suspect the governor is not aware of that fact. Or, if he is, perhaps his bribe was large enough to make it worth the risk."

I gave Erasmus a hard look—but when I saw his sly grin, I ended up laughing instead.

"Don't worry, my friend," he said. "God has plans for you. Our job is to get you safely out of town so you can fulfill those plans. You should be safe here while we finish making arrangements for your escape. Keep the door bolted. When I return, I'll knock like this," and he made a series of taps on a wooden table with his knuckles. "Got that?"

I repeated the pattern of knocks.

"Very good," he said.

*****

About the middle of the next afternoon, I heard Erasmus' knock at the door.

"Who is it?" I asked quietly.

"Erasmus."

I opened the door, and he slipped in.

"Put this on over your regular cloak," Erasmus said as he handed me a dark brown garment. "It's the darkest shade I could find."

"Purpose?"

"It's partly to put you in a color and style different from what you've previously worn, but it's primarily to have you in something that will be hard to see at night."

"Is this the night I attempt my escape?"

"No, my friend; this is the night you *make* your escape."

"What's the plan?"

"Since both the Jews and the soldiers are still watching all the city gates, we must avoid them. The southeastern portion of the city walls are more lightly guarded than the other portions of the wall, partly because there aren't as many watch towers there, and partly because that is the opposite direction from where you normally go.

"A family of believers lives in that part of the wall, and has agreed to allow us to use their home as a part of your escape. If you are ready to go, I will take you there now."

"I'm ready."

Erasmus wrapped an extra cloth across the lower portion of my face, and pulled my head cloth forward a bit so that my entire head was covered by cloth, shadows, or both. Then he stepped back, appraised me for a moment, nodded and said, "Let's go."

We stepped outside and looked in both directions, but saw no one. Erasmus turned left and began shuffling down the road, heading east. I joined him. We crossed to the other side of the street and turned right at the next corner. Now we were going south.

We continued to thread our way through the dusty streets of Damascus, primarily going either south or east, although we occasionally deviated in order to avoid groups of soldiers or Jews whose raiment indicated they were Pharisees, Sadducees, or other religious leaders. Since this was Damascus rather than Jerusalem, there were not many of those.

Eventually we came to an east-west street but turned right onto it, which meant we were walking west instead of east. I looked around, but saw no danger.

Erasmus noted my puzzled look, smiled, and softly said, "We are getting close to our destination. Stay in the shadows next to the walls as much as you can."

He led me to a break between two buildings. We squeezed our way down a narrow pathway that opened into a small courtyard covered with a canopy of limbs and branches from many trees.

"Wait here," Erasmus said.

I waited while he sauntered across the street to an arch in the city wall. At the center of the arch was a door. Erasmus knocked, waited a few minutes, and then knocked again. After a few moments, a man opened the door. Erasmus spoke briefly to him, turned, and motioned for me to come.

I crossed the street and passed through the doorway in the wall. The other man closed and bolted the door by sliding a heavy wooden beam across it. The entryway opened only onto a stone stairway that led up inside the wall. Erasmus and I followed the man up two flights of stairs to an apartment consisting of several rooms that were more or less in a straight line and which comprised part of the outer wall of the city.

Erasmus turned to me and said, "Saul, I'd like you to meet Mark"—and he placed his right hand on the shoulder of the man who had led us up the stairs—"and his wife, Mary." She gave a slight bow to me. "They are both believers, and will be your hosts for at least a few hours. If all goes according to plan, they will let you down through that window an hour or two after midnight."

I walked to the window and looked out. It was narrow enough that it appeared more like a slit or small opening in the wall rather than a window. We were about two-thirds of the way up the city wall. The ground then sloped down to a roadway that ran parallel to the wall.

Erasmus pointed to a grove of trees on the opposite side of the road. "Do you see those trees?" he asked.

"Yes," I answered.

"If there is no change in plans, I will be behind those trees with two black horses at the time Mark and Mary let you down out of this window."

"How will we know whether the plan has changed?" I asked.

"This is a covered lantern. Light the wick inside it and then cover it so that light does not escape. Extinguish all other lights at midnight. I will also have a covered lantern with me. When I see your lights go out at midnight, I will briefly uncover my lantern. When you see my signal, briefly uncover your lantern three times. That way, I will know you saw my signal. Wait an hour or two and then let Saul down out of the window. Any questions?"

All three of us indicated that we understood.

Erasmus left the apartment so that he could make the necessary arrangements. While Mark, Mary and I waited in their apartment, we examined the basket and rope they would use for lowering me to the ground. I briefly got into the basket and made sure I could cover myself and be hidden.

Three other men arrived at the apartment around dusk. I knew Ananias and Benjamin, of course. The third man was Thomas, a believer who attended a different synagogue.

"Does this mean you are also a believer?" I asked Benjamin.

"I think you have probably known—or at least suspected—for some time," the rabbi replied.

"Well, yes, you tipped your hand when you asked Barnabas to read that passage from Isaiah about how the Messiah would suffer and be crushed as a sacrifice for our sins."

Benjamin smiled and patted my back.

We still had several hours until midnight. We used our time to test the pulley attached to the wall above the window, and made sure it, the rope and the basket were all able to work as planned. We then moved a table into position next to the window. Since the table was slightly higher than the bottom of the window ledge, it facilitated pushing a loaded basket through the window. Finally, we loaded the basket with belongings I would take with me when I attempted my escape.

No, these are the possessions I take with me when I **make** *my escape,* I smiled as I mentally made the correction Erasmus had impressed upon me earlier. *The Lord must have a wry sense of humor,* I thought to myself, *or maybe it's a warped sense of humor. The mighty Saul of Tarsus, who originally approached Damascus armed with letters of authority from the governor and the Jewish high priest, is about to be lowered by night in a fish basket . . . being helped by the very people he had originally come to arrest and possibly kill.*

Lamps, lanterns and candles were lit before the apartment got completely dark. One of the candles we lit was a timing candle Erasmus had left us so we would know when it was about midnight.

When that time arrived, we extinguished all lights except the one inside the covered lantern. Since it was covered, darkness enveloped the apartment. We looked out the window.

Nothing happened for a couple of minutes. Then we saw a light briefly flicker in the grove of trees across the road.

Mark uncovered his lantern for a few seconds. He then covered and uncovered the lantern two more times before closing the draperies over the window. We then made final preparations, extinguished all lights, and waited about an hour.

I climbed onto the table, Mark handed me the basket, and I got into it. The cover was secured, and the four men hoisted the basket as well as they could and pushed it through the window.

There was a sickening moment when the basket tumbled away from the window and I feared I would crash to the ground below. Then the ropes held, and I was gently lowered. When the basket came to rest at the base of the wall, I unlatched the cover and climbed out, taking my possessions with me. My companions retrieved the basket, pulled it back through the window, and hid it inside the apartment.

I made my way down the incline to the roadway and crossed over to the grove of trees on the opposite side, where Erasmus was waiting with the horses. We briefly embraced, mounted the horses, and rode together along the road in a southwesterly direction.

Within a few stadia, the road we were following intersected the highway I had originally taken to Damascus. I took special note of the place where I had first encountered the Lord, though it looked different at night. After riding about half an hour, Erasmus turned off onto a small road that intersected from the left, and I followed.

When we came to a house surrounded by sycamore trees, Erasmus rode around the house to a fenced enclosure, where he stopped and dismounted. He opened a gate, led his horse inside, and directed me to do likewise.

"Hafid is part owner of this land," Erasmus explained, "though the business is actually run by the other owner, Judah. We will spend the night here."

When I awakened the next morning, I met Judah and his wife, Elizabeth. Since both of them were also believers, we were able to talk freely about our experiences while sharing breakfast. Erasmus and I thanked them for their hospitality, and then went our separate ways. Erasmus was heading back to Hafid's home outside Damascus, while I would continue on to Jerusalem.

"When you get to Jerusalem, take the horse to Joseph of Arimathea's shipping office," Erasmus said. "He can send it back to us in one of his caravans. Here are enough denarii to cover your expenses for the next couple of months. May God lead, guide, and direct you always."

"Thank you so much for all you and Hafid have done for me," I said. "I don't think I can ever adequately repay you for your kindness."

"We both believe God has great things in store for you. Accomplish his will—and that will be payment enough. *Shalom.*"

"*Shalom.*"

Judah's house was almost due east of Mount Hermon[75] and was in between two major trade routes. I made my way eastward, since that route was less travelled by Jews than was the western road that I had originally taken from the Sea of Galilee to Damascus, and then followed the eastern route southward to Raphana, Abila, and the Decapolis.

I spent the night in Philadelphia, crossed over the Jordan River the next morning, and was in Jerusalem early in the afternoon. As luck would have it, I was able to follow one of Joseph of Arimathea's caravans to his shipping office in Jerusalem. I was excitedly looking forward to meeting Jesus' disciples as a fellow believer. I soon learned they did not share that degree of enthusiasm at the prospect of meeting me.

---

[75] At 9,232 feet (2,814 meters) above sea level, Mount Hermon is the highest point in Syria. It is part of a long ridge or cluster of peaks that helps form the border between Syria and Lebanon.

22.

The caravan I had been following pulled into an enclosed courtyard. Drivers led their camels to troughs of water, and handlers began unloading packs as I quietly rode past. I was unsuccessfully looking for a familiar face when I suddenly heard someone call my name.

"Saul! Is that really you, Saul?"

I reined in my horse and looked around. Joseph of Arimathea was trotting toward me with a massive grin on his face. I dismounted.

"I'm afraid so," I answered. "How are you doing, Joseph?"

"Never better, my friend. Will you be here in Jerusalem long?"

"Hopefully—but this horse doesn't belong to me, and I need to return it to its owner. Do you have any caravans that go through Damascus?"

"All the time, Saul."

"Would you be willing to return this horse to Hafid?"

"That would be no problem. Take your belongings, and I'll see that it's done." Joseph turned to an assistant and told him to take the horse to the stables and give it to a groom there to feed and water. Then Joseph turned back to me and said, "Go into my office and wait for me. I want to visit with you, but must first finish my business here."

When Joseph and I later visited freely and candidly, I told him about the threats on my life in Damascus.

"Let me make certain I understand what you're saying, Saul," Joseph said with a twinkle in his eye. "The reason you came to Jerusalem is that it was getting too hot for you in Damascus. Is that right?"

"Something like that," I replied.

"Isn't that similar to jumping out of the cooking pot and landing in the fire?"

I just looked at him without responding.

"You just got through telling me that the Damascus officials were allegedly bribed by Jewish religious leaders. Have you forgotten that those religious leaders live and work here in Jerusalem? If Damascus was too dangerous for you, what makes you think Jerusalem will be better?"

"You may be right. It might not be any safer for me," I replied. "But this is my second home. I've practically grown up here. I was taught by Gamaliel, welcomed by the Pharisees, admitted to the Sanhedrin, and made plenty of friends in this city."

"Can you really count on those friends any more? The religious leaders who once embraced you—the Pharisees, Sanhedrin, and priests—may very well be the ones who bribed the Damascus officials to have you killed."

"You're probably right. However, I know this city better than any other in the world. If I need to escape, my knowledge of the streets, alleys and other spaces should be an advantage for me. Besides, Jerusalem is where Jesus' disciples live. I want to talk with some of them."

"Which ones?"

"Peter, at least. Maybe James, John, or some of the others."

"I think that can probably be arranged. Do you have a place to spend the night?"

"No, not yet."

"Well, you do now . . . provided, of course, you don't mind staying at my house."

"If that would be all right with both you and your wife."

"Esther? I wouldn't have asked you to come if I thought there might be a problem."

*****

The next Lord's Day, I went with Joseph and Esther to a worship service that was held in the same upper room that

Jesus had used for his last supper with his disciples before being crucified. It marked the first time for me to see the disciples since my encounter with the risen Jesus on the road to Damascus.

As we approached the house, I noticed various groups of people watching us. Some appeared to be rather agitated, while others were merely confused or concerned. When we were about a block from the house, one young man ran to the house. He emerged a few moments later with Peter and John.

John and the young man stood in the doorway to the house, while Peter walked toward us. He placed his hand on Joseph's shoulder and asked to visit with him privately. The two men walked off a short distance to my left and engaged in a quiet but lively discussion. I couldn't hear what they were saying to each other, but they were both using forceful gestures. I gathered that they were strongly disagreeing about something.

After several minutes, Joseph raised both his hands in an exasperated manner, turned and walked back to Esther and me, shaking his head slightly and looking rather upset. He glanced first at Esther and sighed. Then he put his arm around my back and quietly said, "I'm sorry, Saul, but I'm afraid you earned too notorious a reputation while you were trying to destroy the Lord's church."

"What do you mean?" I asked.

"The believers here in Jerusalem are too afraid of you."

"That was three years ago! I've changed since meeting Jesus on the Damascus road."

"I know—and I told Peter that."

"Surely he of all people knows how Jesus can change a person."

"True, true, but they are just too suspicious of you. They suspect you are trying to trick them."

"This is ridiculous," I muttered. "The Jewish leaders are trying to kill me, and the Jewish believers won't let me near them. Where do I turn now?"

"Now?" asked Joseph. "Now we return home and plot another course of action. I have a few ideas that might work."

Joseph stood on the corner thinking for a moment. Then he nodded, smiled and said, "Wait here. I'll be back very shortly."

He turned and walked to the house where the believers were meeting. A few minutes later, he came back to us—but in a much better mood.

"What happened?" Esther asked.

"You'll see," was all Joseph would say.

We returned to their house in Arimathea and ate lunch.

A few hours later Barnabas arrived, and Joseph told him what had happened.

"I'm not overly surprised that the Jerusalem church is still afraid of Saul," Barnabas replied. "After all, he was extremely effective in his efforts to wipe out the church. Many of the followers of the Way lost friends and family as a result of Saul's efforts."

"But Barnabas," Joseph pleaded, "you've spent time with Saul in Damascus and personally know he has changed from being a persecutor of the church to being a driving force for the Lord. Jesus himself chose Saul. That ought to be good enough."

"Joseph, Joseph, you're preaching to me; I need no convincing. As you observed, I have spent time with Saul in Damascus . . . and that's not all. Ananias told me the Lord told him that he had chosen Saul to carry his message."

"Then you'll help Saul?"

"Of course I'll help him. I'll try to set this straight with the disciples. They know me and trust me."

Two days later Barnabas returned and asked me to go with him to a residence in Jerusalem. Although the house was in the upper part of the city, it was still older and smaller than the other structures around it.

Barnabas knocked at the door, and it was opened by Peter.

"Come in," he said.

We washed our feet in the entry way and sat down in the front room. Peter acted as if he felt a bit awkward, but blurted out, "Barnabas has been telling me about your conversion on the Damascus road. He said he spent several weeks with you in Damascus and is convinced you have really and truly changed."

"That's all true," Barnabas said.

"Yes," I added.

"Then I hope you won't mind if I ask you some questions."

"Go right ahead."

After asking several questions that probed what happened, Peter asked, "Is it true that Jesus said he had chosen you to be his messenger to the Gentiles?"

"I don't know," I responded. "He didn't tell me that."

"You got that from me," Barnabas interjected. "When I was in Damascus, Ananias told me that Jesus appeared to him in a vision and told him Saul is his chosen instrument to carry his name and message to the Gentiles and their kings, as well as taking it to the people of Israel. He also said Saul will suffer much in the name of Jesus."

"That first part is what I don't understand," Peter said. "We Jews are God's chosen people. Unless God specifically directs us to take the message to the Gentiles, I think it would be wrong to do so."

"I really can't comment on that other than to say that at this point in time, God has not sent me to the Gentiles," I said. "I have, however, been active in spreading the message in Jewish synagogues . . . and anywhere else I can visit with the lost sheep of Israel."

"Yes, that's what Joseph of Arimathea told me last Lord's Day."

"Why wasn't Saul allowed to worship with us?" Barnabas asked.

"Too many of the Jerusalem believers had their homes disrupted when Saul arrested family members while he was persecuting the church. Quite frankly, they're suspicious—and afraid of you, Saul. You apparently were just too effective in your efforts against the church."

"Suspicious of me? Peter, I haven't arrested, threatened, or persecuted anyone for the past three years—ever since Jesus stopped me in my tracks on the road to Damascus."

"I'm aware of that, Saul. Nevertheless, it would probably be better if you refrain from attending . . . at least for a while."

"What about you, Peter?" I asked.

"What do you mean?

"Are you also afraid or suspicious of me?"

"I'm not sure, Saul. I really don't know you that well—but you seem to have won over both Barnabas and Joseph of Arimathea."

"Would you be willing to get to know Saul better?" Barnabas asked Peter.

"Maybe. What do you have in mind?"

"Let him stay with you for a week or two—provided, of course, that both of you want to do something like that."

Peter and I shifted our gaze from Barnabas to each other. Both of us were silent for a minute or so. Then Peter shrugged and said to me, "I'm willing if you are."

"A fisherman and a tent maker," I replied. "What a combination! Sure, why not?"

I grinned at Peter, and he responded in kind. Barnabas put his arms around both of us and said, "That's the spirit, men!"

All three of us laughed.

23.

While staying with Peter, I asked him, "What was it like being Jesus' disciple?"

"It was the most amazing experience of my life," he replied.

I cocked my head and waited for him to continue—but instead, he got a misty look in his eyes and remained silent for several minutes. It was as if his mind had moved to another time and place, and he was savoring the memory. I also remained silent, watching as conflicting emotions flickered across Peter's face.

"It was . . . incredible . . . absolutely incredible," Peter finally stammered. "He knew things no normal person could know, and he could do things beyond the power of mortal men."

"Such as?"

"Well . . . once while we were crossing the Sea of Galilee, a violent storm suddenly arose and threatened to destroy our little boat. Despite the turbulence, Jesus remained asleep until we woke him. I shook him and shouted, 'Master, Master, we're about to drown!' Jesus got to his feet, calmly walked to the side of the boat, and rebuked the storm."

"What happened?"

"The storm immediately subsided, the howling winds ceased, the raging waves calmed, and the water became peaceful and quiet. Jesus turned to us and asked, 'Where is your faith?' Then he lay back down and went to sleep again as if nothing had happened."

"What did the disciples say or do?"

"We just looked at each other in amazement and asked, 'Who is this? He commands even the winds and the water, and they obey him!'" Peter shook his head as the memory overwhelmed him.

"And that's not all," he continued. "Jesus had a miraculous power to heal people. He could restore sight by touching a blind person's eyes . . . or by mixing his saliva with dirt to make a salve that he placed on their eyes . . . or even by just commanding the blind man's eyes to receive sight. He could similarly heal a lame person's broken or deformed bones . . . or heal various other ailments—all by just saying the word."

"As God spoke the world into existence, so can the Son speak the word to heal broken bodies," I muttered.

"Exactly!" Peter exclaimed. "Jesus could even speak the word that restored life to a dead person."

"Really?"

"Yes. I saw him do it several times. Jairus, the ruler of one of the Galilean synagogues, asked him to heal his sick daughter. As we were going to Jairus' house, we received word that the little girl had died. Jesus went on anyway and brought her back to life. Perhaps the most famous resurrection was when Jesus restored the life of Lazarus, who had been dead four days."

"I heard about that while I was in Tarsus."

"Well, it certainly made quite a stir. Many people were ready to anoint Jesus as the promised Messiah—which may have been the final straw for the religious leaders, who decided they had to get rid of Jesus any way they could."

"What do you think, Peter? Is Jesus the Messiah?"

"Yes. Most definitely."

Peter got a far-away look in his eyes, and silently gazed off into the distance for a moment before continuing, "In fact, I was the one who made that very confession when we were camped near Caesarea Philippi."

"Please tell me about it."

"Have you ever been to Caesarea Philippi?"

"Yes."

"Do you remember all the pagan shrines?"

"Yes, especially those dedicated to Pan."

"Multitudes had been flocking to see Jesus, to hear his teachings, and be healed by him. We retreated to the area around Caesarea Philippi and had been looking at some of the pagan shrines and talking about different beliefs. Jesus asked us who the multitudes said that he was. We responded with some of the most common assertions."

"Such as?"

"Oh, some said that Jesus was actually John the Baptist."

"But John had been killed by Herod, hadn't he?"

"Yes, but quite a few people claimed that he had come back to life as Jesus. Anyway, that was the first name which was mentioned. The disciples also said Isaiah, Jeremiah, and some of the other Jewish prophets."

"What did Jesus say?"

"He nodded his head knowingly, paused, and then asked us who we thought he was. I responded, 'You are the Christ, the Son of the living God.'"

"What was Jesus' response to you?"

"He said, 'Blessed are you, Simon son of Jonah, for this was not revealed to you by man, but rather by my Father in heaven.'"

"So Jesus acknowledged both that he is the Christ or Messiah and that he is the Son of the living God?"

"That he did—and he also gave me the name by which I am now called."

"What do you mean?"

"Jesus used my confession of his identity as an opportunity for making one of his plays on words, of which he was a master."

"What did he do?"

"He continued his blessing by saying, 'And I say that you are Peter, and on this rock I will build my church, and the gates of Hell will not overcome it.'"

My expression must have been rather blank, because after a short pause, Peter asked me, "Don't you get it?"

"I'm not sure."

"And I say that you are Peter—*Petros*, a small rock or stone, and on this rock—*Petra*, a caprock or large stone—I will build my church, and the gates of Hell will not overcome it. I may be as solid as a rock, but much greater and more solid is my confession that Jesus is the Christ, the Son of the living God."

"That confession is the foundation of Jesus' church, the message we have been proclaiming to the world," I said.

"You've got that right, my lad. But the second play on words is that we had been looking at Pan's Grotto adjacent to the Temple of Pan. That grotto is often called the Gates of Hell, since the cavern descends into an extremely deep pit, and the water gushing out of the mouth of the cave forms the headwaters for the Jordan River. I think Jesus was inferring that the pagan religions of this world will not be able to withstand the message we proclaim!"

"I've spent most of the last three years studying prophesies about the Messiah," I said. "Although I'm convinced he is the Christ, there's one thing I don't understand."

"What's that?"

"Although Jesus fulfilled too many prophesies for him not to be the Messiah, there were some that were not fulfilled."

"Which ones?"

"A number of prophesies indicate that the Messiah would sit on the throne of his ancestor David, he would rule his people forever, and would be the all-conquering hero who would lead the Lord's armies as God's vengeance was administered to sinful people who had refused to repent and submit to God."

Peter nodded, smiled, and responded, "Jesus taught us that his current mission was to save his people from their sins. He fulfilled that mission by coming to Earth, living a perfect life so that he could be God's perfect sacrifice, dying as that sacrifice, and rising again to usher in God's new and better covenant. He said he will come again—but next time he will be leading the armies of heaven. That's when the rest of the prophesies will be fulfilled."

"Why didn't the prophets distinguish between the two comings?"

"I don't know, but I suspect it may have been because all these things were in the future to them, and the visions God gave them probably did not distinguish between those events that would occur during the first coming and those that would be fulfilled at the end of the age."

Both of us were silent for a few moments, and then Peter added, "Come to think of it, there was one event that may illustrate what I just said to you."

"What's that?"

"Once, Jesus was visiting a synagogue on the Sabbath, and was invited to read from the scroll of Isaiah. The part he read contained some of Isaiah's prophesies regarding the Messiah.[76] Jesus stopped in mid-sentence and told the crowd, 'Today this scripture is fulfilled in your hearing.' The rest of the sentence—the part he did not read—contained Isaiah's prophesy of something Jesus did not fulfill this time, but will do when he comes again.[77]"

"That's interesting. Thank you for sharing those memories with me, Peter."

A few days later I met Jesus' brother, James,[78] when he came to Peter's house.

---

[76] Isaiah 61: 1-2a. Luke 4: 14-21.
[77] Isaiah 61: 2b.

"Tell me, James," I said. "What was it like to have Jesus as your brother?"

"I'm not really sure how to answer that question, Saul. It was a complex combination of emotions all sliding over each other and sometimes contradicting one another."

"What do you mean?"

"How would you feel if your older brother could seemingly do no wrong?"

"Although I never had an older brother, I imagine it could be exasperating."

"It was, believe me. And it only got worse when he left home and started preaching and teaching."

"Why's that?"

"Several reasons. For one thing, he was no longer around to earn a living, help with the housework, and look after Mother. We had also relied upon him for more things than we wanted to admit—such as his advice and guidance. But the worst things were probably the crowds following him and all the people claiming he might be the promised Messiah or even the Son of God."

"Wait a minute!" I interjected. "I thought you believed in him. Don't you also consider Jesus to be both the Messiah and God's Son?"

"I do now—but I resisted it until after his resurrection."

"Why?"

"Put yourself in my place, Saul. What would be your reaction if your own brother claimed to be either God or the Son of God?"

"I'd probably think he was delusional . . . or crazy . . . or worse," I laughed.

"Exactly! And that's what my siblings and I tried to tell ourselves at first. I think deep down I knew there was

---

[78] Although it might technically be more accurate to list James as Jesus' half brother, the Bible calls him "the Lord's brother" when this incident is mentioned in Galatians 1:19.

something very special and unusual about Jesus. He had always been too good to be true . . . but God? Come on! How many times had we been taught in Hebrew school that there is only one God?"

"More times than I can count," I answered. "When did you start to change your feelings—to move toward believing in him as your savior?"

"Again, I probably had always realized there was something different about Jesus that I just couldn't explain. Then one day I overheard Mother talking to some man—and she told him about how she had been approached by an angel who had informed her she was going to give birth to the Messiah . . . and that her son would be called the Son of God.

"I didn't want to believe it. I wanted the Messiah to be a great military hero who would free us from Roman rule—rather than being a brother whose advice was to turn the other cheek. It was easier to think of Jesus as being crazy for even entertaining such thoughts. So I tried to fight it . . . tried to deny that it could possibly be true. But I sometimes slipped off and watched Jesus from a distance as he healed people and preached to them. He had a power I couldn't explain. I began to wonder if it could really be true.

"Then he was crucified on a Roman cross. What a horrible way to die! When I heard the news, I was stunned—shattered. Mother had gone to Jerusalem by herself. I knew she would be even more devastated—so I hurried to Jerusalem and tried to find her.

"I eventually found her living with one of Jesus' disciples named John. But instead of being wiped out by Jesus' death, Mother was in good spirits. She claimed that Jesus had been resurrected and was alive again. I thought she was delusional—until I met the risen Jesus."

James' eyes locked onto mine, and his jaw quivered as he said, "Jesus really and truly is the Christ, the Son of the living God! When I broke down and confessed what I knew to be true, it was as if a terrible burden had been lifted from my soul. I almost felt as if I could fly and soar to the heavens above!"

"Exactly!" I exclaimed. "I know the feeling. The risen Christ confronted me on the road to Damascus, took away my sight for three days and forced me to see the truth. When I finally accepted him as my Lord and savior, I felt as if I were floating on air; my soul had been set free. It was the most exhilarating feeling I've ever experienced."

James smiled, nodded his head, and said, "I guess both of us were initially opposed to the idea that Jesus could be the Messiah, much less the Son of God."

"Yes, it was a long and difficult road for us to move from being opposed to Christ to being evangelists for him."

We embraced—and only later realized that both of us had tears flowing from our eyes.

24.

I stayed with Peter for fifteen days. Although I did not attend any more of the Lord's Day services with the other believers, I went to the temple and to various synagogues, where I boldly proclaimed the good news that Jesus had come to seek and to save the lost sheep of Israel. I declared that Jesus was the perfect sacrifice foretold by Isaiah.[79] He died to save us from our sins, was resurrected by God almighty, and had ascended to heaven.

One day I encountered a group of Grecian Jews who adamantly claimed I was speaking falsely. "The only thing you said that is true and correct is that Jesus of Nazareth died on a cross. I know that is true because I was there and saw it myself," one of them proclaimed.

"All that I said was true," I replied. "Why do you think otherwise?"

"Under the covenant God made with his chosen people, we are to bring a lamb without spot or blemish as our sacrifice, and God will accept the blood of the lamb as a substitute for the sinner's blood."

"That's true." I said.

"However, God has not only rejected human sacrifice, but he has said that such sacrifice is an abomination to him, and he finds its stench repugnant to him."

"Agreed."

"Yet you claim that Jesus of Nazareth willingly offered up his own life as a blood sacrifice for our sins. In other words, you claim he was a human sacrifice."

---

[79] Isaiah 53.

"You make an interesting argument," I conceded. "However, you need to remember that both Jeremiah and Ezekiel said God would make a new and better covenant[80] than the one you referred to. The new covenant would be written on people's hearts rather than on stone, would be everlasting, and it would be as if the people had been given new hearts for God.[81]

"Although the lambs that were sacrificed pursuant to the old covenant may have physically been without spot or blemish, they were not tempted in all ways as we are, yet resisted such temptations so as to be without sin. That is what is required in order to be the perfect sacrifice.

"Only a person can be so tempted—but no person can resist all such temptations, since all have sinned and come short of the glory of God. Therefore, God himself had to provide the perfect sacrifice by coming to Earth, living among us and being tempted as we are but without yielding to such temptations.

"This is the Messiah's true purpose: Not to lead human armies against human foes, but rather to defeat the forces of Satan and darkness; to save his people from their sins so that they may have an everlasting relationship with God."

"You are claiming then that almighty God came to Earth as Jesus?"

"Yes—most emphatically yes!" I replied joyously.

He looked at his two Hellenistic Jewish companions and said, "I don't think I've ever heard such outrageous blasphemy!"

"Nor have I," replied one of the others.

"We cannot allow such unmitigated blasphemy to go unpunished!" the leader asserted. "Grab him; kill him!"

The man on my left lunged for my left arm. As he grabbed it, I immediately swung that arm across the front of

---

[80] Jeremiah 31: 31-34; Ezekiel 16: 60-62, 37: 26.
[81] Jeremiah 31: 33-34; Ezekiel 11: 19, 16: 60-62, 36: 26-27, 37: 26.

my body. His momentum joined with my arm movement, and caused him to stumble in front of me. As he fought to keep his balance, I turned my head toward him and butted the side of his head with my forehead. He released my arm and staggered forward a step. I slammed my left elbow into the same spot on his head, and the man's legs folded up under him as he collapsed to the ground.

I then turned toward my second assailant just as he lunged toward me from my right. I instinctively jerked my right arm upward while folding my hand into a fist back against my chest so that my right elbow became a wedge pointed toward the man's face. He slammed into my elbow with a sickening thud that broke his nose and sprayed my arm with his warm, sticky blood.

The impact knocked me backward, but otherwise left me intact except for the blood across my right side. The second man's momentum carried him forward and downward. I helped him along by chopping the back of his neck with my right hand, and he crumpled to the ground.

"You are a marked man!" the leader shouted at me. "There are seven more of us here in Jerusalem. When we find you, we'll kill you."

"May God's peace be upon you as well," I responded. Then I turned and walked back to Peter's house.

"What happened to you?" Peter exclaimed when he saw me.

"Some Hellenistic Jews objected to what I had to say about Jesus."

"Is that your blood or theirs?"

"Theirs."

"I thought you had reformed, Saul, and had ceased your violent ways."

"Peter, I was attacked by several of them. One of them charged into my elbow and broke his nose. The bruise on my forehead came when I butted heads with another attacker."

"You hit him with your forehead?"

"Yes."

Peter shook his head and then quipped, "You always were good at using your head."

"A Roman centurion once told me a man's forehead can be a formidable weapon. He said it was much thicker than the side of the head—so I used mine against the side of the other man's head."

"It's a good thing you're as hard-headed as you are."

"I may have to be if they carry through on their threats."

"What do you mean?"

"Their leader said there were seven more of them—and that they would find me and kill me."

"Do you think he was serious?"

"Deadly serious."

"In that case, we must get you out of here as quickly as we can. Grab your possessions; you're coming with me."

Peter led me to Barnabas' house, and then the three of us went to Joseph of Arimathea's shipping office. Later that day we joined one of his caravans, headed for Caesarea on the coast of the Mediterranean Sea.

When we stopped for the night, I had a chance to visit with Peter and Barnabas before going to sleep.

"While we were traveling, I had a chance to reflect on some of the things you told me earlier," Peter said to me. "It's been approximately three years since you were converted on the road to Damascus. What did you do during that time?"

"I primarily studied the scriptures," I replied.

"Why . . . and what did you find out?"

"I thought I had good training as a result of my Jewish education—especially that portion when Gamaliel was my teacher. I had a solid foundation in Jewish law and tradition, and thought I was following God's leadership and commands when I was persecuting the church.

"Then I encountered Jesus while on the Damascus road. Suddenly I discovered that my beliefs and thought patterns were wrong and misguided. Instead of being a warrior for God, I was actually fighting against him. I needed time and study to determine where I had gone so wrong. I needed to know what God was trying to teach me."

"What did you learn?"

"I discovered that God has replaced his old covenant with Israel with a new and better covenant with the believers who constitute the church. The old covenant was largely founded upon the Law of Moses, while the new one centers upon belief in Jesus Christ as our Savior, redeemer and mediator. God's grace is evident and essential in both covenants. But while the law is primarily useful for showing us how unworthy we are of God's grace, it also left us with a depressing realization that we must forever offer sacrifices to God in order to be forgiven of our ever-present sins."

"Is that why the Pharisees and other religious leaders always seem to have such long faces and be in such a rotten mood?" Barnabas asked.

I looked at him with a questioning gaze, not sure whether he was being serious. Although his big brown eyes were twinkling, he did not appear to be joking. "I don't know, Barnabas . . . but you may have something there."

"Well, don't you know? After all, you *are* a Pharisee—and a religious leader of the Jews."

"What makes you think that?" I asked.

"You're a member of the Sanhedrin; what else would you call it?"

"I haven't been active or attending the Council since Jesus converted me."

"Still, you should be in a position to know."

"As I said, you may be correct. We may never know whether we have kept all aspects of the Law in conformity with God's requirements. If we have failed in any portion, we have sinned and fallen short of what the Law mandates.

If we think we have kept all the Law's requirements, we tend to get smug and proud of our accomplishments. And pride itself can be a sin."

"In other words, there is little joy in merely keeping the Law."

"Precisely—which might justify those long faces and rotten moods you mentioned."

Peter laughed and slapped Barnabas on the back.

"On the other hand," I continued, "under the new covenant, our debt has been paid in full by Jesus Christ. We have been covered with his righteousness, and now stand in his debt for our redemption and salvation."

"Which means?" Barnabas prompted.

"Which means we have a joy that bubbles up from our inner being that others have difficulty in comprehending," I said.

"What does that do to those long faces and rotten moods?"

"It positively abolishes them!" I exclaimed. "It's hard to maintain a rotten mood while thinking about how much God loves us . . . and all that he's done for us."

*****

When we arrived in Caesarea, we left the caravan and walked to the port facilities, where we located a ship which was about to sail for my old hometown of Tarsus. I purchased a ticket and said my farewells to Peter and Barnabas.

I was able to sit by myself for extended periods of time while on the boat, and I used that time to reflect on the dramatic changes that had occurred in my life since I left Tarsus a few years earlier. The man who I thought was one of my best friends had recruited me to go with him to Jerusalem to hunt down and arrest the people who believed Jesus was the Christ, the son of the living God. Now I was one of those believers—and it was my friend who was now hunting me.

I had been admitted to the Sanhedrin, proof that I was considered to be the brightest and best of my age group. Shortly before his death, my father told me how proud he was of me. Would he still feel that way? What surprised me was that I really was not particularly concerned with that thought. Instead, I found myself aching that I had not had an opportunity to tell my father about Jesus, to witness to him, and to help him know the truth about the wonderful liberating power that can set the soul free.

I also realized that another force was at work in my life. I had always taken pride in my own personal abilities and independence. My intellect and reasoning abilities had enabled me to be not only accepted by the great Gamaliel as one of his students, but to become his personal friend. Even as a very young man, I had been admitted into the rarified company of Jewish religious leaders that comprised the Pharisees and the great Sanhedrin. I was repeatedly told that God had great things in store for me; I was marked for greatness.

The high priest himself personally chose me to head up the task force that sought to find and destroy the followers of Jesus, although we were not permitted to arrest Jesus' disciples, since too many people turned to them for healing. Nevertheless, I was given letters of authority from both the high priest and the Roman governors.

It was while I was attempting to carry out my marching orders pursuant to those letters that everything suddenly changed. When confronted by the living and resurrected Jesus, I had to admit that his followers were right—and I had been wrong.

But that admission had other implications as well. My exalted intellect and reasoning had led me to the wrong conclusion. My powerful allies in the religious community were actually fighting against God—and I had been helping them. And the ones who came to my aid and helped me the most were most often lesser known individuals like Ananias,

Rachel, and the other believers who yielded to the Holy Spirit's instructions and leadership even when they could not rationally understand why they should do so.

As I prayerfully reflected on the changes God had been making in my life, I realized that he had even been molding and modifying my independent spirit. When I was growing up, I had been encouraged to be my own man, to follow my own instincts and conclusions, and to lead the way toward whatever course I had determined to be correct without depending upon others.

My training and education only intensified my independent spirit. People told me I would be a valuable tool and asset for God—and I believed them. Unfortunately, those comments tended to stroke my pride. Even after God brought me to an abrupt halt on the road to Damascus and turned me totally around, the knowledge that the Lord had personally appeared to *me* and had chosen *me* to be his instrument for reaching the Gentiles and their rulers encouraged my independent spirit and filled me with pride.

I couldn't wait to get started in my new mission of winning the lost for Christ. Yet God seemed to keep allowing roadblocks to get in my way; obstacles kept blocking my path. Even after I slowed down and took three years to study the scriptures, I was still prevented from debating and preaching in both Damascus and Jerusalem. Why? What was I doing wrong . . . or what was God trying to teach me?

By the time the ship I was on sailed into the harbor near Tarsus, I had concluded that God is not as interested in rewarding pride and arrogance as he is in blessing humble people who realize they are unable to either save themselves or to complete the job of evangelizing by themselves; they need God and his miraculous grace. I needed to totally surrender myself to God's will and his leadership. I needed God to take over and to give me his direction and the strength to get the job done. In other words, I needed to learn to lean on God, to trust in him, and to wait; I needed to put my independent spirit into the hands of God and let him mold me according to his will.

Too long had I felt that I was the captain of my soul. I needed to humble myself and let the Lord be the captain. I needed to realize that I was his slave.

I trod up the dusty road to Tarsus with the firm resolve to wait for the Lord to show me his will; I was finally content to allow God to direct my path. I had no idea that would be one of the hardest things I had ever done, since my impatience and old independent spirit kept attempting to rise up and take control once more. But God saw fit to leave me on the sidelines at Tarsus for several years. I used the time to think through the scriptures and their application, to prayerfully formulate a consistent doctrine . . . and to learn to wait on the Lord—to wait until God's perfect time had materialized.

25.

A knock at the door. I looked up and said, "Come in."

"Saul?" a man asked as he hesitantly entered. "Is that you?"

The raspy voice sounded vaguely familiar, but I couldn't immediately determine where I had previously heard it. "Yes," I answered. "That's my name. May I help you?"

A man of average height who appeared to be about my age stepped through the door. His large brown eyes sparkled mischievously while studying me. His mouth crinkled in a wry grin as he asked, "Don't you recognize me?"

I squinted my eyes, momentarily racked my brain, and then gasped, "Barnabas! Is it really you?"

We embraced—or rather, we took turns embracing and holding each other at arm's length while we each eagerly examined the face of a friend we had not seen for several years.

"It's been . . . what . . . five, maybe six years?" I asked.

"I think so. At any rate, too long, my friend."

"What brings you to Tarsus?"

"I've been looking for you, Saul."

"For me? Why"

"Do you remember Antioch?"

"The city?"

"Yes."

"Of course, though I haven't been there in years."

"Have you heard the news about what's been happening there?"

"Not that I recall."

"Well, let me tell you. I was sent there by the Jerusalem church."

"Why?"

"The Spirit of God has been working there in a mighty way, and many people—both Jews and Gentiles—were being saved through the preaching of some believers from Cyprus and Cyrene. Since I was originally from Cyprus, the disciples in Jerusalem sent me to Antioch to see for myself what was happening.

"What I saw positively amazed me. I witnessed the grace of God working in a mighty way. Well, naturally I was heartened by what I saw, and encouraged them all to remain true to the Lord and to continue spreading the good news of the gospel.

"Large numbers of people are coming to the Lord each week. In fact, there's way too much happening there for us to handle. We need help. We need you!"

"Me?"

"Yes, you. You're not too busy, are you?"

"Look around, Barnabas. I've been largely sitting here by myself, making tents to earn money—but otherwise marking time until the Lord decides to use me."

"That doesn't sound much like the Saul I thought I knew."

"In many respects, it isn't. The Jews here flogged me and eventually cast me out of their synagogues. Once I was beaten so badly that I lapsed into a trance. While in that state of mind, the Lord gave me a vision . . . possibly even transported me to Paradise and revealed amazing sights to me.[82] It's been hard for someone as ambitious and restless as I have always been, but I have finally learned to wait for the Lord to lead and guide me. Does your coming here mean that God is ready to use me?"

---

[82] 2 Corinthians 12: 2-7.

"Yes, Saul. Now is the time. Come with me to Antioch."

"You said large numbers of people are coming to the Lord there. What people?"

"Some Jews . . . but most are Gentiles."

"I thought the disciples in Jerusalem opposed taking the gospel to Gentiles."

"Well, that's true—at least initially . . . but when Peter explained what happened in Caesarea . . ."

"Wait . . . wait . . . hold it!" I interrupted. "Peter? Caesarea? When you and Peter took me to Caesarea to put me on the ship to Tarsus, Peter was the one who was most opposed to sharing the gospel with Gentiles."

Barnabas stood mute in front of me for a moment with a surprised expression on his face. Recognition slowly registered as he seemed to remember past history.

"That's right," he agreed. "You left before Peter's vision or the Holy Spirit's descent upon the Gentiles."

"The what?" I exclaimed.

"Sorry, Saul. You've been out of the loop longer than I remembered. I need to fill you in on what's been happening."

"Please do."

"After Peter and I left you in Caesarea, he visited the believers in several nearby towns, including Lydda and Joppa, where he stayed for quite some time with a tanner named Simon. About noon one day, Peter was praying while lunch was being prepared. I don't know whether it was because he hadn't eaten yet, but Peter began dreaming about food."

"Yeah, I often do that when I'm especially hungry, too," I quipped.

"Actually, this was more of a trance than a regular dream. Peter had a vision of heaven opening and something like an enormous sheet being lowered down to him. The sheet contained all kinds of four-footed animals, as well as reptiles and birds. Peter heard a voice tell him, 'Get up, Peter. Kill and eat.'

"'Surely not, Lord,' Peter replied. 'I have never eaten anything impure or unclean.' Peter heard the voice respond to him, 'Do not call anything impure that God has made clean.'

"The vision repeated a second time . . . and then a third time. Each time Peter protested that he had never eaten anything impure or unclean—and each time the voice from heaven told him not to call anything impure that God has made clean.

"Peter awoke, but with full memory of having had three identical visions. As he sat at Simon's house wondering what the visions could possibly mean, a knock was heard at the front door. Men from Caesarea were inquiring whether a Simon who was also called Peter was there in the house.

"Peter was still upstairs thinking about the three visions when the Holy Spirit informed him, 'Simon, three men are looking for you. Get up, go downstairs, and talk with them. Do not hesitate to go with them, for I have sent them.'

"Peter went down and said to the men, 'I'm the one you're looking for. Why have you come?'

"They replied, 'We have come from Cornelius the centurion in Caesarea. He is a righteous and God-fearing man, who is respected by all the Jewish people. A holy angel told him to have you come to his house so that he could hear what you have to say.'

"Naturally, Peter and Simon invited the men into the house to be their guests."

"Naturally," I replied. "Then what happened?"

"The following day Peter left for Caesarea with the three men sent by Cornelius—but he took with him several other Jewish believers from Joppa. When they got to Caesarea, they discovered that a large number of people had gathered at Cornelius' house to hear what Peter had to say.

"Peter said to them, 'As you probably know, it is against our law for a Jew to associate with a Gentile or visit him in his home. But God has shown me that I should not call any man impure or unclean. So when I was sent for, I came without raising any objection. But I still do not know why you sent for me.'

"Cornelius answered, 'In the middle of the afternoon four days ago, I was in my house praying when a man in shining clothes suddenly appeared before me and said, "Cornelius, God has heard your prayer and remembered your gifts to the poor. Send to Joppa for Simon who is called Peter. He is a guest in the home of Simon the tanner, who lives by the sea." So I sent for you immediately, and it was good of you to come. Now we are all here in the presence of God to listen to whatever the Lord has commanded you to tell us.'

"Peter replied, 'I now realize that God does not show favoritism, but rather accepts men from every nation who honor and worship him and do what is right. You know the message God sent to the people of Israel, telling the good news of peace through Jesus Christ, who is Lord of all. You also know what has happened throughout Judea and Galilee, beginning after the baptism that John preached—how God anointed Jesus of Nazareth with the Holy Spirit and power, and how he went around doing good and healing people because God was with him.

"'We are witnesses of everything he did; we were with him as he taught us, loved us, and died for us. Yes, the Jews in Jerusalem killed him by hanging him on a tree, but God raised him from the dead on the third day and caused him to be seen by many people. He commanded us to preach to the people and to testify that he is the one whom God appointed as judge of the living and the dead. All the prophets testify about him that everyone who believes in him receives forgiveness of sins through his name.'

"While Peter was still speaking to the Gentiles in Cornelius' house, the Holy Spirit suddenly came on all who heard the message. The circumcised Jews who had come with Peter were astonished that the gift of the Holy Spirit had been poured out on even the uncircumcised Gentiles. Tongues of fire lit on them and they began speaking in tongues—just as had happened to us at Pentecost—and everyone was praising God.

"Then Peter asked, 'Is there any reason not to baptize these people with water? They have obviously received the Holy Spirit just as we have.' No objection was made by any of the Jews, who all agreed with Peter. After the Gentiles were baptized, Peter stayed there several additional days."

"What did the Jerusalem church have to say about that?" I asked.

"At first they were highly critical of Peter. When he returned to Jerusalem, they confronted him with their accusations, saying, 'You went into the house of uncircumcised men and ate with them.' Peter responded by telling them everything that had happened . . . just as I've told you. When he got to the part describing how the Holy Spirit had descended upon the Gentiles—even before they had been circumcised or baptized—the Jerusalem Jews were amazed. They had no further objections. Instead, they praised God and said, 'So then, God has granted even the Gentiles repentance unto life.'"

"I firmly believed it was only a matter of time before he did so," I said.

"Why's that?"

"Don't you remember God's covenant with Abraham?"

"I remember—but am not sure I see how that applies to converting Gentiles."

"Part of the covenant was that all the nations on earth will be blessed through Abraham's descendants.[83] God

---

[83] Genesis 22: 18.

made essentially the same covenant with Jacob.[84] Almost all the nations on earth are Gentile, but God promised they would be blessed because of descendants of Abraham and Jacob. I think this was one of the primary missions of the Messiah, Jesus of Nazareth."

We had been walking along the road from Tarsus to Antioch, but Barnabas stopped in his tracks, put both his hands on my shoulders and said, "I think you're right, Saul. Why hadn't I realized that before now?"

"I have no idea. It wasn't exactly hidden."

"No, but I guess I hadn't thought through the implications. But then again, that's one of the things that set you apart from the rest of us who were students of Gamaliel . . . which, of course, is one reason I need you to help us in Antioch."

"Tell me more about what's happening there—and how you got involved."

"You may have been at least indirectly involved."

"Me?" I asked. "How do you figure that?"

"One of the side effects of your strong persecution is that believers were scattered across the Roman world. A number of them ended up in Cyprus and Cyrene, and established churches there. Some Jewish men from there went to Antioch not long after Peter and I put you on that boat to Tarsus, and they witnessed to both Jews and Greeks, and many people accepted Christ as their savior.

"When news of what was happening in Antioch reached Jerusalem, the church there sent me to Antioch to work with the new believers, to evaluate the situation, and to report back to Jerusalem. I was both discouraged and encouraged by what I saw in Antioch."

"What do you mean?" I asked.

"The city of Antioch as a whole is a moral quagmire."

"Quagmire?"

---

[84] Genesis 28: 14.

"Yes," replied Barnabas. "A quagmire often looks inviting—but it can be dangerous or fatal. It's often almost impossible to extract oneself from a quagmire once a person starts sinking in it. Similarly, the corruption of Antioch tends to pull people down until they drown."

"All right," I said. "I can see the analogy . . . though I think *moral cesspool* might be a more fitting term."

"Well, Antioch's morals *are* filthy, corrupt and disgusting. It's a sprawling city of a half million people where crime, gambling and prostitution are rampant. Few places in the Roman empire have more corruption in their government and business practices. The temple dedicated to the goddess Daphne is a place where countless souls join themselves in immoral debauchery with the temple prostitutes. Yes, you're right," Barnabas conceded. "*Cesspool* might be a better term. At any rate, I was discouraged with the overall moral climate of the city.

"On the other hand, I was extremely encouraged by what God is doing there. The gospel is spreading almost like wildfire. People who have participated in Antioch's debauchery have found its pleasures to be fleeting and its promises to be empty; they want something that actually satisfies their souls. Other people have recoiled from the depravity they witness around them and seek the genuine joy that the Lord provides.

"Although many Jews live in Antioch, most of the converts are Gentiles who have little or no knowledge of the scriptures that form the foundation for our beliefs. Thus, large numbers of people need in-depth instructions in Jewish scriptures and traditions as well as personal counseling and teaching about God's expectations and commandments regarding morality and righteousness.

"I realized I was not properly equipped to handle these challenges by myself. When I prayed about the situation, the Lord kept reminding me of your remarkable abilities—which is why I have reached out to you."

"Thank you for thinking of me," I replied. "I hope your faith in me is justified—and I pray that God can use me to advance his kingdom."

26.

I found Antioch to be just as Barnabas had said. This mighty city of approximately half a million people was hungry for the good news of God's love and redemption. Barnabas and I worked tirelessly with the local believers. In fact, we made so much headway in transforming the pagan population that followers of Jesus of Nazareth became known as *Christians* (in other words, *little Christs*) by the people of Antioch.

Although we continued to call ourselves people of the Way at first, gradually the term *Christian* gained acceptance so that even we eventually embraced it. Rather than being offended by being referred to as being a diminutive Christ, I personally regarded it as a compliment, since I hoped others could see my Lord and Master reflected through me and my actions.

I had been ministering in Antioch for about a year when Agabus, one of our Christian brothers from Jerusalem, stood up in one of our meetings and said, "The Holy Spirit has shown me that a severe famine will spread over the entire Roman world, but it will be especially devastating to our brothers in Judea."[85]

"Did the Spirit show what we should do?" asked Barnabas.

"Yes," replied Agabus. "We should send whatever aid and assistance we can provide."

The believers in and around Antioch pooled their resources, set aside some provisions to help the local Christians meet their needs during the coming famine, and

---

[85] This famine occurred during the reign of Claudius.

then sent the rest to the church in Jerusalem so that they could better weather the hard times that were coming. Barnabas and I were selected to take the gifts to the elders in Jerusalem.

When we arrived, we found the believers huddled together behind locked doors, fervently engaged in prayer. James, the brother of John and the son of Zebedee, had been publicly executed by King Herod.[86] When he saw how much James' death had pleased the Jewish religious leaders, Herod arrested Peter and put him in prison, where he was guarded by four squads of soldiers.

"Peter is scheduled to stand trial tomorrow," John explained to me, "and it is a foregone conclusion that the trial will end with a guilty verdict and a death sentence. That is why we are earnestly praying to God for him."

Barnabas and I joined our Christian brothers in asking the Lord to deliver Peter from certain death. We had been praying for a couple of hours when we heard a knock on the door at the outer entrance to the house. Rhoda, a servant girl, went to the door and cautiously asked who it was. She came running back to where we were praying and exclaimed, "Peter's at the door!"

"You're out of your mind!" replied John Mark, who lived in the house where we had gathered for prayer. Several others chimed in with similar comments.

"No!" Rhoda insisted. "I recognized his voice. It really is Peter!"

"It must be his angel," replied John Mark.

"I tell you, it really is Peter!" she said.

"If it really was Peter, where is he?"

Rhoda and Mark stopped shouting at each other and looked toward the front door. The incessant knocking

---

[86] This Herod was the son of Aristobulus and Princess Mariamne, and was the grandson of Herod the Great. He was named king by Roman Emperor Gaius Caligula.

continued. Rhoda went back to the door and opened it. To the astonishment of the believers who had been praying for his release, Peter himself stepped into the house and motioned for them to be quiet.

John rushed up to Peter and embraced him. "How in the world did you get out?"

"Sit down and I'll tell you."

We gathered around Peter, and Rhoda brought him some food to eat while he talked.

"I was bound with several chains, sleeping between two guards in prison when I felt a jab in my side. I groggily looked up and saw an angel of the Lord standing before me. 'Quick, get up!' he said to me. He touched my wrists and the chains fell off.

"'Put on your clothes and sandals,' the angel told me. When I had done so, the angel took a step back and said, 'Wrap your cloak around you and follow me.' I did as the angel instructed, but I didn't really realize that it was actually happening; I thought I was merely dreaming all this . . . or possibly having a vision.

"We walked past guards and sentries who apparently were unable to see us, which added to my feeling of unreality. As we approached each cell door, it would open and we would pass through. The door would then close and lock behind us. The last door we passed through was the big iron gate leading to the city. When we walked through it, the cool breeze of the night hit my face; I fully awakened and became aware that I was on the street outside the prison. The angel led me down one street. Just as we got to the end of the street, the angel vanished from my sight.

"At that moment I realized without a doubt that the Lord had sent his angel to rescue me from Herod's clutches and from everything the Jewish religious leaders were anticipating. I decided to come here to Mary's house—and you know the rest."

"We have been praying for your release," John Mark said.

"Well, it obviously worked," Peter replied. "Tell James[87] and the other brothers who aren't here about this."

"Aren't you going to stay?" asked Barnabas.

"No. I need to get away from here before Herod discovers I am no longer in his prison," Peter said as he embraced several of us. Then he slipped away into the night.

We continued visiting among ourselves about the miraculous way God delivered Peter from Herod's prison. We also wondered what Herod's response would be when he discovered Peter had escaped. Would he realize that his actions were contrary to the will of Almighty God—or would he become angry and intensify his persecution of the church?

We didn't have long to wait to discover Herod's response. When Peter's absence was discovered the next day, a thorough search was made for him throughout Herod's prison. His chains were still in place and were anchored to the wall, but the prisoner was missing! All the doors were properly locked, and none of the guards reported seeing anything out of the ordinary. Since Peter had been chained between two guards, those soldiers were personally cross-examined by Herod himself—and when they could not explain how Peter had escaped, Herod ordered that they be executed.

Barnabas and I stayed in Jerusalem for several days. During that time Barnabas introduced me to many of our Christian brothers there. It was my first opportunity to freely visit with them, since they had been afraid of me during my earlier times in Jerusalem. The Jerusalem believers were most grateful for the generosity of their

---

[87] This James was the brother of Jesus. The James killed by Herod was one of Jesus' disciples.

counterparts in Antioch—even if they were primarily Gentiles.

John Mark and his mother, Mary, were especially interested in hearing about the explosive growth of the church in Antioch. Mark had a keen thirst for learning, and he had a reputation for being curious. Some of Jesus' disciples claimed that on the fateful night when Jesus was betrayed by Judas, Mark had followed them to Gethsemane . . . wearing nothing but a linen garment. They said that one of the soldiers arresting Jesus grabbed hold of the linen—and Mark had run away naked, leaving his garment behind.

Mark was still curious. He continually pestered us with questions. Finally Barnabas told him, "Well, why don't you go back with us and see for yourself?"

"May I? May I? Would it be all right?"

We looked at his mother. She thought for a few moments and then said, "If it's all right with both Barnabas and Saul, I have no objection. It might be safer than being here at this time. Who knows what Herod might do next?"

Thus it was that when Barnabas and I returned to Antioch, John Mark came with us. We thought he could spend some time in a new and different city that would be interesting for him while still being safe from persecution. We had been in Antioch long enough that we thought we knew what to expect. Little did we know that the Lord had other plans for us.

27.

While we were worshiping the Lord and fasting one day, the Holy Spirit said, "Set apart for me Barnabas and Saul for the work to which I have called them."

Barnabas and I looked at each other questioningly, not sure what the words and instruction meant.

Lucius of Cyrene stood up and told us, "Kneel here before us, brothers."

We kneeled where he indicated, and all our Christian brothers gathered around us. One by one, each of them placed his hands on us and prayed for us. While they pooled their provisions and took up an offering to help us, we remained in earnest prayer, seeking guidance from the Holy Spirit.

Barnabas wanted to go to places where large numbers of Jews lived, while I advocated taking the gospel to the Gentiles. After long prayer sessions over the next two days, both Barnabas and I felt very strongly that the Lord wanted us to journey to the island of Cyprus, which had a sizeable Jewish population that had already been exposed to the Christian gospel message—but also had many Gentiles. We hoped the Lord would then give us a sign or directive as to where we should go next.

"Are you just going to leave all this?" John Mark asked us.

"What do you mean?" I responded.

"Well, look around us. I'm not sure I've ever seen such excitement. People are flocking to the church here in

Antioch. They are ravenously hungry for the gospel. Your teaching and Barnabas' encouragement have really met people's needs here—and they are responding. I don't see how you can turn your backs on all this just as it is fully blossoming."

For once, I was at a loss for words. Since I wasn't sure how to respond, I just stood there with my mouth open. Luckily, I didn't have to answer Mark; Barnabas did it for me.

"Yes, Mark. In a way, I agree with you. What God is doing here in Antioch *is* exciting. I am thrilled to see all the changed lives and rejoicing that is occurring here. Lucius, Simeon, and Saul may have planted a wonderful crop here, and Manaen and I may have watered it with our encouragement and leadership—but it is God who is really responsible for the tremendous growth."

"That's right," I chimed in. "And it is God who is now directing us to go elsewhere. The important thing is for us to remain in his will and under his control."

"So God is now telling you it's time to move on?" Mark asked.

"Yes. Didn't you feel the Holy Spirit's direction? I know I did," I said.

"Well, I *thought* I felt something, but I'm not sure it was as clear for me as it seemed to be for the rest of you."

"It was clear to me," Barnabas responded. "The Spirit spoke . . . and we listened. And not just us; the others here in Antioch also knew that they needed to release Saul and me to follow the Spirit's leadership. Isn't it great to have a fellowship that is so in tune with God's will that we can immediately follow his leadership and direction?"

"I . . . guess so." Mark was silent for a moment. Then his face brightened and he said, "That's what I want, as well."

"What's that?" asked Barnabas.

"I want to learn to follow God's direction and know his will for my life."

"That's good."

"May I go with you?" Mark asked.

Barnabas looked at me.

I shrugged and said, "I don't know. The Spirit asked the fellowship to set us aside for his mission. He didn't say anything about John Mark going with us."

Barnabas smiled his wry grin. "But then again, the Spirit also didn't say Mark couldn't come with us."

"I don't have strong feelings one way or the other," I responded. "If he wants to come and won't be in the way—and if you want him to come along, then it's fine with me."

"I would also like to go with you," a doctor named Luke said. "You never know when you might need a doctor, and I have been gathering information about Jesus and his church. I'd appreciate being able to travel along with you and take notes."

"What kind of notes?" I asked.

"I'll show you," Luke responded, and he showed me a papyrus scroll. Notes had been scribbled on the scroll about our activities in Antioch.

"Isn't papyrus expensive?"

"Yes, but I can afford it—and it takes up much less room than wax tablets."

"Doctor Luke has been interviewing most of the disciples and other key people about the life and ministry of Jesus," Barnabas explained to me.

"What key people?" I asked, looking at both Luke and Barnabas.

"Jesus' mother, Mary. All of Jesus' disciples. For that matter, I also travelled with them on occasion, and I listened to many of Jesus' teachings and personally saw many mighty miracles," Luke said.

"Why?"

"Initially, I was intrigued by Jesus. He had a power and a purpose that transcended anything I had seen. The more I watched, the more I was drawn to him. I hope to write an orderly manuscript about the life of Jesus, including the major teachings of Jesus."

"That's fascinating." I looked at Barnabas and asked, "Can you vouch for him?"

"Absolutely!"

"Then by all means, come along. I want to hear about some of the things you've learned."

28.

We walked from Antioch down to Seleucia, where we boarded a boat and sailed to Salamis, the primary commercial center and port on the eastern half of the island of Cyprus, which had a sizable Jewish population. Since Barnabas was a Cypriot, he was familiar with the island and led the rest of us to the Jewish quarter of Salamis, where we found lodging.

On the Sabbaths, we went to the Jewish synagogues. We visited with various individuals and groups of people throughout the rest of each week, sometimes using the power of the Holy Spirit to heal people with various infirmities. After several weeks in Salamis, we set out on foot across the rest of the island. We hiked from village to village, sometimes walking throughout the night to get to the next town.

We eventually arrived in the southwestern port city of Paphos. Again we went first to the Jewish synagogues, but also spent time proclaiming the good news of the gospel to others we met.

However, we had not been long in Paphos before we were summoned by the proconsul or governor of the province,[88] Sergius Paulus, to meet with him at his palace. I

---

[88] Rome took over Cyprus in 57 B.C., and the island was given to the Roman Senate as a gift by Augustus in 22 B.C. The Senate appointed Sergius Paulus as Rome's proconsul, and he governed the island in the name of Rome.

was excited to have the chance to preach the gospel to the Roman governor.

The governor's palace was an impressive edifice constructed of gleaming milk-white stones with matching stately columns that formed the entry way, which was adorned with beautiful mosaic pictures. One of the mosaics depicted Aphrodite, the Greek goddess of love and beauty, as she rose from the sea—which reminded me that Greek mythology claimed that Aphrodite was born near this site, and the great temple dedicated to that goddess was located here. With pagan mythology being so prevalent, I wondered how open Sergius Paulus would be to the gospel message.

Immediately prior to being introduced to the proconsul, I decided to use the Latin version of my name rather than the Hebrew version I had used up to that point in time. Therefore, instead of being called *Saul* at the palace, I was introduced as *Paul* . . . which was similar to the governor's name.

Unfortunately, I found it difficult to preach the gospel or even to answer Sergius Paulus' questions because of constant interruptions and heckling by the court magician or sorcerer, a Jew known as Elymas, who called himself Bar-Jesus.[89] I put up with it as long as I could—actually quite a bit longer than I can normally abide fools or scoundrels.

I felt the power of the Holy Spirit fill me as I turned toward that turncoat Jew and said, "You call yourself Bar-Jesus—the Son of Jesus—but you are actually a child of the devil and an enemy of everything that is right and honest! You are full of all kinds of dishonesty and accomplish your 'magic' and 'sorcery' through slight-of-hand trickery and deceit. Will you never stop perverting the right ways of the Lord?

---

[89] Elymas means "wise" in Arabic, while Bar-Jesus means "son of Jesus" in Hebrew.

"Now the hand of the Lord is against you," I said as I raised my arm and pointed my index finger at him. "You are going to be blind; for a time you will be unable to see the light of the sun."

Immediately mist and darkness came over Elymas, and he groped about and exclaimed, "What have you done to me? I can't see! How dare you do this to me?" He tried to charge toward me, but tripped and fell. Finally a guard helped him up and led him by the hand out of the room.

The proconsul had previously been mildly interested in the gospel, but now he was raptly enthralled. He eagerly asked questions, and we answered them. Before we left his palace, Sergius Paulus made a profession of faith in Jesus Christ.

Barnabas and I had hoped and prayed for a sign regarding whether to go to areas populated almost entirely by Gentiles and their pagan religions. When this Gentile Roman official believed, we had our sign: The door to the Gentiles had opened before us!

29.

"You earlier told me that you had interviewed quite a few people about Jesus," I remarked to Luke as we rocked along in a boat headed from Cyprus to Perga in Pamphylia.

"That's true," Luke responded.

"You also said that one of those people was Mary, Jesus' mother."

"Yes."

"What did she have to tell you?"

"She talked about Jesus' birth . . . and his death . . . and some incidents in between."

I waited silently for Luke to continue. After a moment he nodded, smiled, and said, "Mary told me she was a teenage girl living in the Galilean town of Nazareth when an angel named Gabriel appeared to her."

"Appeared . . . how? In a vision?"

"No. Gabriel apparently physically appeared to her and said, 'Hail, favored one; the Lord God Almighty is with you!' Since Mary was both confused and frightened, the angel reassured her by saying, 'Do not be afraid, Mary, for you have found favor with God. You will conceive in your womb and bear a son, and you are to call his name Jesus, for he will save his people from their sins. He will be great, and will be called the Son of the Most High. The Lord God Almighty will give to him the throne of his father David. He will reign over the house of Jacob forever, and of his kingdom there will be no end.'"

"So Gabriel told Mary her son would be the promised Messiah."

"That's right," Luke confirmed. "But his words confused Mary even more. She couldn't understand how she could have a baby, since she was a virgin. She was promised to a local carpenter named Joseph; although they had been through the *Eyrusin* betrothal ceremony, they had not yet consummated their marriage, and both were still virgins. Mary therefore asked Gabriel, 'How can this be, since I am a virgin and have no husband?'

"The angel answered, 'The Holy Spirit will come upon you, and the power of the Most High God will overshadow you. Because the Lord God Almighty will use a part of his own Spirit to impregnate you, the Holy One who is to be born will be called the Son of God.' Gabriel also told Mary that her kinswoman Elisabeth—who was thought to be barren and too old to get pregnant—had also conceived a son in her old age, for nothing is impossible with God."

"What was Mary's response?"

"She bowed her head and said she was the handmaid of the Lord; she would do what the angel requested."

"What happened next?" I asked.

"Mary decided to verify what Gabriel had told her. She went to see Elisabeth—and discovered that Elisabeth was six months pregnant. Mary stayed there until the baby was born and then returned to Nazareth . . . but by this time, she was also pregnant!

"Mary met privately with her betrothed, Joseph. As you might imagine, Joseph was devastated by the news. He said he couldn't believe that Mary was the kind of woman who would have sexual relations with any other man after entering into a Hebrew *Eyrusin* betrothal. Joseph reminded Mary that after they participated in the ceremony, they were considered married even though they continued to live separately until the end of the betrothal period.[90] They

---

[90] Jewish betrothals usually lasted from one to fifteen months, with most being about a year long.

were expected to keep themselves sexually pure throughout that time.

"Joseph seemed even more disappointed that Mary apparently couldn't believe in him enough to tell him the truth, and instead had invented such a far-fetched story. Mary ran home crying, and earnestly prayed that God would take control of the situation."

"Did he?"

"Apparently, since Joseph met with Mary the next day and told her what had happened since he had last seen her. He said he had thought and prayed all the previous day, and had finally decided to quietly divorce Mary rather than making a public example of her. However, that night, an angel of the Lord appeared to him in a dream and said, 'Joseph, son of David, do not fear to take Mary as your wife, for that which is conceived in her is of the Holy Spirit. She will bear a son, and you are to call his name Jesus, for he will save his people from their sins.' When Joseph awoke, he did as the angel had instructed him, and took Mary as his wife. However, they refrained from having sexual relations until after Jesus was born."

"So both Mary and Joseph were living in Nazareth?"

"That's right."

"Then how is it that Jesus was born in Bethlehem?"

"That's an interesting side story," Luke said. "Caesar Augustus decided to levy a new tax on all the people across the Roman Empire, but he first needed to conduct a census so he would know approximately how many people there were and where they were located. However, instead of conducting the census of the people where they lived, he decided to make all the people return to their ancestral homes. Since both Joseph and Mary were of the house and lineage of King David, they were therefore required to travel to the City of David—Bethlehem—just as Mary was about to give birth!

"When they got to Bethlehem, they discovered there was no room for them. Not only was the local inn filled beyond its capacity, but the local citizens had already taken in as many travelers as they could. Even their relatives living in Bethlehem had filled their guest room. Luckily, the innkeeper took pity on them (primarily because of Mary's condition) and allowed them to stay in a nearby cave he used as a stable for his animals.

"Joseph placed the cleanest straw he could find in the manger used as a feed trough for the stable animals. When Jesus was born, they wrapped him in some soft clothes they had with them, using the manger as a makeshift crib.

"Later that night a group of shepherds appeared at the mouth of the cave and asked permission to enter. They said they had been sent by angels, who informed them that the Christ child had just been born in Bethlehem. The shepherds said they were terrified by the sight of the heavenly host and the glory of God that filled the landscape around them. Consequently, they immediately did what the angels had suggested, and found the baby in the manger. After gawking at Jesus for a few minutes, they nervously left—but Mary noticed they were glorifying and praising God as they went.

"Mary told me she was glad the shepherds had come by, since that may have helped Joseph to accept that what Mary had told him about the angel and being impregnated by God was really the truth. Having total strangers show up claiming that the angelic hosts of heaven had announced the birth of the Christ child probably helped dispel any lingering doubts."

"Thank you for sharing that with me, Luke," I said. "You also said she shared her thoughts about Jesus' death with you."

"Yes. Mary told me how bitter and confused she was as she stood before the cross watching her miracle child die. She said she thought back to Gabriel's announcement that she had been chosen by God to bear the promised Messiah who would save his people. She had willingly allowed herself to be used for God's mission, even though it meant people would spread vicious rumors about her and talk about how she had been unfaithful to Joseph. When he had taken her as his wife anyway, the gossip had changed to make him a party to the shame of not waiting until marriage to be sexually intimate with each other. When they had returned to Nazareth after Jesus' birth, the gossipers resumed making their snide remarks.

"It had not been an easy life, but Mary had willingly and even joyfully done her part. However, seeing her son cruelly nailed to a Roman cross, broken and bleeding, eyes puffy and body covered with caked blood, was more than she could bear. Making it even worse were the gloating, mocking and derisive insults hurled at Jesus by the people who surrounded the crosses.

"God had promised Mary that the child she bore would be the long-anticipated Messiah who would save his people. Mary had always believed that God was trustworthy and kept his promises—but as she stood before the cross, Mary couldn't understand how God could let it all end that way. Jesus had never hurt anyone. In fact, he had spent his entire life helping and healing, encouraging and lifting people up. Mary knew she should trust that God knew best, but she couldn't see how Jesus' crucifixion fulfilled Gabriel's promise. What was the purpose? Where was God's justice? How could the Lord let this happen?"

"Did she ever get answers to her questions?"

"Yes—but not until after the resurrection. I'm happy to say that her doubts and questions have been settled, and she has gladly accepted her son as her Lord and savior."

*****

When we made port at Perga in Pamphylia, we discussed where we should go first. I expressed a desire to head toward Pisidian Antioch, a Roman colony near Pamphylia's border with Pisidia.

John Mark took a long look toward the rugged terrain we would have to cross to get to Antioch and seemed to wilt. "This trip has already been rougher than I had bargained for," he said, "and I miss my home in Jerusalem much more than I thought I would. I think I should head back."

"What?" I exploded. "You asked to come along with us, and we let you. You've been a good help thus far. You have real potential to be a vibrant force for the Lord—provided that you press forward and don't quit. I don't see why you suddenly need to run back home to your mother."

Mark bristled and clamped his teeth together to keep from saying something he might regret later. "Sorry," he muttered between clenched teeth.

"It's late in the day," Barnabas said. "Why don't we get something to eat, spend the night at a local inn, and then see how everyone feels in the morning?"

However, since Mark seemed even more resolutely set on returning the next morning, we put him on a ship bound for Jerusalem, and let him go. Barnabas, Luke and I then set out for Antioch of Pisidia. We had no time to waste if we were to make it before the Sabbath.

30.

The road to Pisidian Antioch led across rugged mountainous terrain—and we were on foot. I had contracted some type of coastal fever or food poisoning[91] that slowed me down and made it harder for me to keep going. I was thankful to have Doctor Luke with us, since I might not have been able to press on without his assistance.

By the time the town came into sight, our bones were aching and our muscles were weary. Nevertheless, since we were on a mission for our Lord, we pressed on . . . and got to Antioch shortly after sunrise on the Sabbath. We wearily made our way to the local synagogue and sat down. After reading from the Law and the Prophets, the rabbi who was leader of the Antioch synagogue noted there were several visitors present. He then turned to us and said, "Brothers, if you have a message of encouragement for the people, please speak."

Naturally, that was more than enough invitation for me. I stood up and gestured toward the Jews and Gentiles in attendance as I said, "Men of Israel and you Gentiles who worship God, listen to me! God chose our forefathers as his special people. He made the people prosper, helped them endure their time as slaves in Egypt, and then used his mighty power to deliver them from that country.

"God endured their conduct in the wilderness for about forty years. He overthrew seven nations in Canaan and gave

---

[91] Possibly [m]alaria.

their land to his people as their inheritance. After this, God gave them judges until the time of Samuel the prophet.

"When the people asked for a king, God gave them Saul, son of Kish, who ruled forty years. Next God made David king and said, 'I have found David to be a man after my own heart; he will do everything I want him to do.'

"From this man's descendants God has brought to Israel the Savior and Messiah Jesus, as God had promised through his prophets. Before Jesus came, John the Baptist preached repentance and baptism to all the people of Israel. As John was completing his work, he said, 'I am not the Messiah, but he is coming after me. I am not worthy to untie his sandals, but I willingly prepare the way for him.'

"Brothers, children of Abraham and you God-fearing Gentiles, it is to us that this message of salvation has been sent. The people of Jerusalem and their rulers did not recognize Jesus as being the Messiah—yet in condemning him they fulfilled the words of the prophets that are read every Sabbath.

"Though they found no proper grounds for a death sentence, they asked Pilate to have him executed. When they had carried out all that was written about him, they took him down from the cross and laid him in a tomb. But God raised Jesus from the dead, and for several weeks he was seen by many people, who are now witnesses to our people.

"We tell you the good news: what God promised our fathers he has fulfilled for us, their children, by raising up Jesus. As it is written in the second Psalm: 'You are my Son; today I have become your Father.'[92] The fact that God raised him from the dead, never to decay, is stated by Isaiah in these words: 'I will give you the holy and sure blessings promised to David,'[93] and is foretold by the psalmist when he wrote, 'You will not let your Holy One see decay.'[94]

---

[92] Psalm 2:7.

"For when David had served God's purpose in his own generation, he fell asleep; he was buried with his fathers, and his body decayed . . . but the one whom God raised from the dead did not see decay.

"Therefore, my brothers, I want you to know that through Jesus the forgiveness of sins is proclaimed to you. Through him everyone who believes is justified from everything, which could not be accomplished under the Law of Moses. All men and women can be justified by faith in Jesus Christ and given freedom that was not possible under the old covenant.

"But I have one word of warning. Take care that what the prophets have said does not happen to you: 'Look, you scoffers, wonder and perish, for I am going to do something in your days that you would never believe, even if someone told you.'"[95]

As we left the synagogue, the people invited us to speak further about these things on the next Sabbath. Many of the Jews and the devout converts to Judaism followed us out and asked us questions about what I had said. They also urged us to return and tell them more.

When we came back a week later, we discovered the synagogue was filled to overflowing. It looked as if the entire city had turned out to hear what we had to say. Since a large number of the visitors were Gentiles, many of the Jews in attendance were offended . . . and some of the Jewish leaders were jealous.

They glared at us and said loudly, "Who do these men think they are, to come in here and stir up the people like this? We graciously allowed them to speak to us last week—but how do they repay our kindness? They bring in all this

---

[93] Isaiah 55:3.
[94] Psalm 16:10.
[95] Habakkuk 1:5.

Gentile scum so that we—God's chosen people—do not have a decent place to sit!"

"Not only that," complained another of the Jewish leaders, "but they present a condemned criminal as being God's promised Messiah. If he truly were the Christ, shouldn't he have led his rebellion against Rome by now?"

Other Jews shouted their agreement and also talked abusively against the gospel I had presented to them a week earlier. I waited for several minutes to see if the abusive language would be answered by those who had encouraged us to return. When it became clear to me that the Jews had apparently decided not to listen to what we had to say, I stood up, motioned for quiet, and said, "We felt we had to speak the word of God to you first."

Barnabas added, "I am extremely sorry that you have apparently chosen to reject God's message of grace, reconciliation, and salvation."

"But since you reject it and do not consider yourselves worthy of eternal life, we now turn to the Gentiles," I said. "For this is what the Lord has commanded us: 'I have made you a light for the Gentiles, that you may bring salvation to the ends of the Earth.'"[96]

When the Gentiles heard this, they stood up and cheered. We walked out of the synagogue and were followed by the Gentiles in attendance. In a nearby meadow, we explained the gospel message to the crowd that gathered to hear us. The Gentiles appeared glad to hear the word of the Lord, and many of them believed and accepted Christ as their savior. We continued preaching and teaching daily to all who gathered to hear us, and the body of believers formed a church and made plans to worship regularly together.

The jealous Jews of the synagogue continued their campaign against us and our message. They complained

---

[96] Isaiah 49:6.

about us to the city authorities and other leaders, who forcibly expelled us from the city. We responded by shaking the dust of the town's streets from our feet in protest, turned our backs on Pisidian Antioch, and journeyed to Iconium.

As we trudged eastward toward our next destination, my anger gradually subsided. At first my blood seemed to boil as I thought about the outrageous conduct of the Jews in Pisidian Antioch. I decided to ask the Lord for guidance and direction—and was astounded by the result. Instead of telling me how to wage a massive counterattack against my foes, he reminded me of his own experiences on the cross. While he was suffering one of the most torturous forms of execution ever devised by the warped minds of men, our savior prayed for the men who were reviling and taunting him. It was God's love for humanity that really held Jesus to the cross, not the nails that pierced his wrists and feet.

If he could go through the excruciating pain and suffering of crucifixion, surely I could endure the indignities we had suffered thus far. I was ashamed that I had been angry, and asked God to grant me additional patience, love, and empathy for those who opposed us. By the time we got to Iconium, I could hardly wait to preach to more Jews at their synagogues.

"Children of Abraham and God-fearing Gentiles," I said to those attending the Sabbath synagogue service, "when the Lord challenged Abram to leave his country and go to the land God would show him, the Eternal One made a covenant with Abram. He said, 'I will make you into a great nation and I will bless you; I will make your name great, and you will be a blessing. I will bless those who bless you, and whoever curses you I will curse; and all peoples on earth will be blessed through you.'

"Later, God changed Abram's name to Abraham,[97] and later still he renewed his covenant. The Lord told Abraham,

'I swear by myself that because you have not withheld from me your son—your only son—I will surely bless you and make your descendants as numerous as the stars in the sky and as the sand on the seashore. Your descendants will take possession of the cities of their enemies, and through your offspring all nations on earth will be blessed.'

"Jeremiah prophesied that the time is coming when God would make a new and better covenant. The Lord said, 'I will put my laws in their minds and write them on their hearts. I will be their God, and they will be my people. No longer will a man teach his neighbor, or a man his brother, saying, "Know the Lord," because they will all know me, from the least of them to the greatest. I will forgive their wickedness and will remember their sins no more.'[98]

"By calling this covenant *new*, God made the first one obsolete, and what is obsolete will soon disappear. Indeed, the first covenant has been fulfilled by the promised Messiah, who has come and has instituted the new and better covenant promised by Jeremiah.

"Under the old covenant, we had to present imperfect sacrifices of sheep as atonement for our sins. We were the ones who sinned; we were the ones who deserved to die—but God was willing to accept the blood of lambs as a substitute for our blood. Since those lambs were never tempted as we were, they were not perfect sacrifices, and we had to continually sacrifice additional animals to atone for the additional sins we continually committed. But it served as a model—a picture—of what God planned to accomplish with the new covenant.

"Under the new covenant, God himself presented the sacrifice on our behalf. You see, only God can live a perfect life without sinning. Thus, only God could be the perfect sacrifice. But since God is eternal, he could not die. How

---

[97] *Abram* means exalted father, while *Abraham* means father of many.
[98] Jeremiah 31:31-34.

could he become the sacrifice needed to redeem us forever? Fortunately for us, God found a way. He did it by using his Holy Spirit to impregnate a virgin; the son she bore was able to live a sinless life, teach us during that lifetime, and then die as the perfect sacrifice for all who believe in him and accept him as their Lord.

"This is the true mission of the Messiah: to save us so that we can have eternal fellowship with God. Jesus Christ is the mediator of a new covenant, and those who accept him as their savior may receive the promised eternal inheritance . . . now that he has died as a ransom to set them free from the sins they have committed. It is by God's grace that we are saved through faith in Jesus Christ."

I paused and looked over the crowd at the synagogue.

"Tell us more," shouted a hearty fellow off to my right. "Are you saying the Messiah has already come?"

"That's correct," I replied. "Jesus of Nazareth is the one who was foretold by the prophets."

"But I thought the Messiah would sit on David's throne and rule his people forever."

"He will—when he comes again," I said. "But don't forget the other prophesies about the Messiah that say he will give his life to pay the debt for our sins."

"What prophesies are you talking about?"

"Isaiah, Zechariah, and the Psalms all say that the Messiah would be rejected by his people,[99] would be struck and beaten,[100] would remain silent in the face of false accusations,[101] would be scorned and mocked,[102] would be led like a lamb to the slaughter,[103] would be smitten,

---

[99] Psalms 22:6; Isaiah 53:3, 8;
[100] Isaiah 52:14; 53:5, 7-8.
[101] Isaiah 53:7.
[102] Psalms 22:7,17; 69: 19-20; Isaiah 50:6.
[103] Isaiah 53:7, 10.

afflicted and pierced,[104] and would thirst and be offered vinegar.[105]

"The Psalms also tell us that people would divide his garments among themselves and cast lots for his clothing,[106] and would pierce his hands and feet[107] but without breaking any of his bones.[108] People would hurl insults at him, saying that since he trusts in God, let the Lord rescue him.[109]

"Because it was the Lord's will to crush him and cause him to suffer as a guilt offering, Isaiah said he would be stricken for the transgressions of his people, and he would be buried in a rich man's grave.[110] However, he would not be abandoned in the grave, nor would God allow his body to decay.[111]

"It was necessary for the Messiah to suffer in order for him to serve as a guilt offering for our sins so that we might be redeemed and have peace.[112] Jesus fulfilled all these prophesies."

Both Jews and Gentiles crowded around me and asked questions—and many of them put their faith in the Lord before the day was out. However, some of the Jews opposed our message, and did their best to turn the rest of them against us. Consequently, both the synagogue and eventually the whole city became divided. Many eagerly accepted Jesus as their savior, but a comparable number vigorously opposed us.

The Lord gave us sufficient courage to continue preaching in the face of opposition, and we were rewarded

---

[104] Psalms 22:16; Isaiah 53:4-5, 7; Zechariah 12:10.
[105] Psalms 22:15; 69:21.
[106] Psalms 22:18.
[107] Psalms 22:16.
[108] Psalms 34:20,
[109] Psalms 22:7-8.
[110] Isaiah 53:9-12.
[111] Psalms 16:10.
[112] Isaiah 53:5-6, 10-12.

when the Holy Spirit gave us the power to heal people miraculously—which earned us the reputation of being able to work wonders and miracles . . . and strengthened the confidence of the new believers in Iconium.

It is said that discretion is the better part of valor—and so it was with us. When we found out that the Jews and Gentiles who opposed us were preparing to stone us to death, we decided it was probably a good time to move on down the road. We continued preaching the good news throughout that region, including in the towns of Lystra and Derbe.

In Lystra we encountered a man who had been born with crippled feet and had never been able to walk. He was raptly listening to me as I was speaking to a group of people. When the Holy Spirit revealed to me that the man had accepted Christ as his savior and could be healed, I looked straight at the man and shouted, "Stand up and walk!"

The man immediately rose to his feet, steadied himself, and took a few steps. "I can walk!" he jubilantly exclaimed as he walked and jumped around. When the crowd saw what had happened, they yelled out in the native language of Lycaonia, "The gods have turned into humans and have come down to us!"

The people decided that Barnabas was really Zeus and that I was Hermes, because I did most of the talking. Since the temple of Zeus was near the entrance to the city, several men ran to it and told its priest that Zeus and Hermes had come in human form to Lystra.

I continued trying to tell the people about Jesus, but they seemed much too excited to really listen to what I was saying. I heard a commotion coming from the city gates—and discovered that the priest from the temple had brought some bulls and flowers to the gates—and was offering a sacrifice to Zeus and Hermes in our honor.

Barnabas and I looked at each other with horrified expressions. We both tore our clothing and ran to the crowd shouting, "Why are you doing this? We are human just like you. Please give up all this foolishness. Rather than sacrificing to men or idols, turn to the living God, who made the sky, the earth, the sea, and everything in them. In times past, God let each nation go its own way. But he showed that he was there by the good things he did. God sends rain from heaven and makes your crops grow. He gives food to you and makes your hearts glad."

Even after we had pleaded with the people, they continued trying to offer a sacrifice in our honor, since they remained convinced that we were gods despite our denials.

While all this commotion was going on, some Jewish leaders from Antioch and Iconium arrived and began stirring up the crowd against us. In a surprisingly short time, the same people who had hailed us as gods grabbed me and dragged me out of the city, where they hit me with stones until they thought I was dead.

Barnabas and Luke gathered over my bleeding body and began earnestly praying for me. I opened my eyes and looked at them. They excitedly helped me sit up. Luke checked my wounds, and said he needed to move me to a place where he could treat them. They helped me to my feet, and we began walking back toward Lystra.

"Do you think it is really safe to go back into a city which just tried to kill you?" Barnabas asked.

"I've never cowered before bullies," I responded. "Besides, I firmly trust God to protect us. After all, we are on his mission—and his Holy Spirit commissioned us to make this trip."

"I need to treat Paul's wounds as soon as possible," Luke added.

The three of us therefore walked back into the city—right past the altar with smoldering remains of firewood that had been prepared for the bulls that were to be sacrificed in my honor . . . while I was allegedly a god.

Luke doctored my wounds, and the next day we journeyed to Derbe, where we won more people to the Lord. We helped the new believers start a church in one of their homes. We then went back to Lystra, Iconium, and Pisidian Antioch. In each town we encouraged the followers of Christ and begged them to remain faithful.

When some of the believers commented on how much hardship we were experiencing, we responded, "We have to suffer much before we can get into God's kingdom. But remember that our savior loves us enough that he voluntarily suffered much more for us."

Barnabas and I chose some leaders for each of the churches. Then we fasted and prayed that the Lord would take good care of these leaders.

We went on through Pisidia to Pamphylia, where we preached in the town of Perga before continuing to Attalia, where we boarded a ship and sailed to Antioch in Syria, since that was where we had been placed in God's care for the work we had now completed.

31.

While we were sailing to Antioch, I reconstructed our missionary journey in my mind and meditated on what lessons God may have had for us to learn. God's Holy Spirit called Barnabas and me and sanctified us for the mission. Even though we had been threatened with death and I had been stoned and left for dead, I was constantly aware of the Spirit's presence, power and protection.

We were granted the power to miraculously heal people—or in the case of Elymus, the power to blind or punish wrongdoers. Healing people of their infirmities obviously helped them and was worthwhile in its own right—but it was also a sign that we had the hand of an unseen power behind us, and generally helped confirm the truth of our message . . . though it could be misconstrued, I wryly thought to myself as I thought about the Lystrans' attempt to deify us.

We had begun the missionary journey on the island of Cyprus, where there was a sizeable Jewish population and the Christian message was already known, since it was a familiar haven for refugees from my own persecution of the church. But Cyprus was also where the Roman governor invited us to his palace, listened to the gospel, and then accepted Christ as his savior. It was there that we felt that the Lord had fully opened the door for us to preach the good news to Gentiles.

Nevertheless, we still presented the gospel to the Jews first in each city we visited before taking it to the Gentiles.

Although a good number of Jews responded to the gospel message, there were others who violently opposed the word of God. It reminded me of my own opposition before Jesus stopped me in my tracks and turned me around.

The Gentiles, on the other hand, were more likely to respond with eager acceptance. Many of them had tried the empty promises and practices of mythology and pagan religions; they realized the futility of praying to man-made objects or inventions. Although the pleasures of pagan temple prostitutes might be tempting, it was also degrading and unfulfilling.

I suspect that we have been created in such a way that we have a natural longing that can only be satisfied by having a viable relationship with God. Until we establish that relationship, we have an empty feeling that we desperately want to fill. People try to satisfy it with material possessions, sex, drugs, various earthly pleasures, religion, work, or other activities or substances. Although they may find temporary relief, the emptiness is still there until the Lord fills it.

Jews have long had a relationship with God under the old covenant, but it was only a prelude to what the Lord had in mind. Although the emptiness may have been at least partially filled by obtaining some relationship with God, that relationship had to go through an earthly priest, and was subject to all the guilt associated with being unable to fully keep all aspects of the Law.

Now that God has initiated the new and better covenant, we can experience a joy and fulfillment that was not possible under the Law and the old covenant. Since Christ serves as not only our savior but also as high priest and mediator, we have been set free to have a gloriously radiant relationship with God that was not previously possible. Jesus fully paid our sin debt provided we accept him as our savior—at which point he also becomes our high priest and mediator so that we can go directly to the throne of God with our prayers and petitions.

If I—a Jew who had a relationship under the old covenant and Law—can know such a wonderful difference under the new covenant and God's grace, just imagine the magnitude of the difference a Gentile may experience going from empty pagan rituals to the fullness of God's grace and glory! No wonder the reception we received from Gentiles was so much greater!

I have been using the name *Paul* instead of my Hebrew given name of *Saul*. As I thought about our experiences, I realized that my change of name may be an admission that I have finally accepted God's purpose and assignment for my life: I am to be a missionary primarily to the Gentiles rather than to other Jews. Rather than being sad about losing my given name, I have readily embraced my new name, Paul. I wryly thought about how God had changed Abram's name to Abraham, and Jacob's name to Israel. Well, why not? It worked for them; maybe it would for me as well.

But the exuberance I felt from sharing the gospel to people starving for the good news was tempered by the memory of the disappointment I felt when John Mark deserted us. He came from a good devoted family. It was their home that had become a central part of the Jerusalem church ever since Jesus had chosen its upper room as the place where he would share his last supper with his disciples immediately prior to the crucifixion.

John Mark had started our missionary journey with such high hopes and enthusiasm. It's good to have hopes and dreams—but hopes are not always fulfilled, and dreams can fade under the harsh glare of reality and life experiences. And really, the opposition we experienced prior to his departure was minimal compared to what happened the rest of the way.

Granted, the coastal mountains we were about to cross were steeper and more intimidating than anything he had seen before. But it was also more rugged than anything Barnabas or I had faced during our lives—and yet we pressed on. Perhaps he was too young and inexperienced to make a trip this arduous and far from home. Perhaps he merely got homesick.

Whatever it was, John Mark gave up and left. I need to remember that people we depend upon sometimes leave us or quit the ministry. But Christ's ministry is greater and more enduring than any person or even a group of people. The church will go on, and the gospel message will continue to be told.

Despite his desertion, we pressed on—and I'm thankful we did. We were able to overcome obstacles like my sickness, rugged terrain, Jewish opposition, pagan superstition, and even being stoned by an angry mob. We showed we could persevere despite frightful obstacles.

One reason we were able to overcome all obstacles was that we never focused on our troubles or earthly measurements like fame or fortune. Rather, we remained focused on our mission and objectives. We constantly reminded ourselves that a lost world was waiting . . . and that it desperately needed to hear the good news. Consequentially, we seized whatever opportunities we were given to speak and share Christ's message.

Finally, we were able to return to many of the places we had visited earlier. This gave us a chance to encourage and strengthen our new Christian brothers and sisters. We planted viable churches and helped them choose leaders who would continue the ministry after we had left the area.

Despite all the hardships and opposition of jealous Jews and superstitious Gentiles, we were able to see the hand of God in all we did. The Lord led and guided us, and he protected us. I may have preached and Barnabas may have encouraged, but it was God who brought the increase to his kingdom.

As I think back on this first missionary journey, I am left with an intense gratitude for all God has done for me and my friends. He rescued me from going the wrong direction with the wrong goals, turned my life around, showed me his unbelievably abundant grace and love, and filled my life with purpose, direction and love.

What a great God we serve!

If you enjoyed
Saul's Quest, read on for a preview of

Joseph's Quest
Overcoming the Obstacles And Challenges of Life

by Bill Kincaid

Chapter 1

Joseph lay at the bottom of a pit. His head and left shoulder hurt from where they had collided with rocks on his way down. Blood oozed from a gash in his left arm. His voice was hoarse from screaming for help. But mostly he was shocked, dazed and scared.

He had initially been upset, angry and incredulous that his own brothers would even think of attacking him. *How dare they do such a thing? Boy, will they ever catch it when Dad finds out! I can't wait to tell him. He'll fix them. Revenge will be sweet!*

But as he considered his fate and his limited options, fear replaced disbelief, though the desire for revenge and the shock of it all remained in full force. *Throwing me into this pit is a serious enough offense they might think they can't afford to let Dad find out. What if they just leave me here — or worse. They could kill me. No one would ever know. Dad didn't know they had left Shechem and come up here to Dothan.*

Joseph's brothers had stripped him of the ornamented tunic he had been wearing, leaving him almost naked when they threw him into the pit. "Stupid!" Joseph muttered to himself. *It was stupid of me to wear that tunic. I knew they were jealous of me for being Dad's favorite son — and wearing that multicolored coat just emphasized to them that I get preferential treatment.*

From where he lay at the bottom of the abandoned cistern, Joseph could hear his brothers talking as they ate. "What should we do with dreamer boy?" one of them asked. Joseph perked up to hear their words better.

"Reuben said for us not to shed his blood," someone else answered. The voice might have been Judah's, but Joseph wasn't sure.

"Yeah, but Reuben's not here now. What if the kid gets out of the pit and snitches on us again?" *Ah, that sounds like Dan.*

"He won't get out," another said. "Simeon tied up his hands real good."

"I agree. Simeon's knots hold."

"But we're talking about Joseph. He might dream up some way of getting out."

"Ha! Dreams!" a brother laughed. "That's what helped put him in that pit."

"Let's see how well his dreams turn out if he dies down there."

Joseph drew in a quick breath. *That was another stupid thing I did. Actually, several stupid things if you count the various times I boasted to my brothers about my dreams of their bowing down to me. Did I really think they would be positively impressed by being told such things? Dumb!*

Joseph turned so he could look up at the cistern walls. The roots and jagged rocks that extended from the sides might offer places where he could wedge hands or feet. But the walls sloped inward toward the narrow opening at the top of the cistern, and his hands were tied in such a way they were almost useless. Joseph looked around for something to use as a knife—but found nothing.

He did hear something, though: His brothers were talking excitedly. At first their words were too quiet for Joseph to understand. But as he strained to catch the words, he heard one brother exclaim, "Yes, I'm sure it's a caravan of camels coming from the direction of Gilead—probably Ishmaelites headed for Egypt."

"Listen, brothers. I've got a great idea."

"What is it, Judah?"

"What do we gain by killing our brother and covering up his blood? After all, he is our brother, our own flesh."

"Yeah—but what do you have in mind?"

"Come, let us sell him to the Ishmaelites. That way we make money, and we don't do away with him ourselves."

"Yeah. His blood won't be on our hands, and we also get paid."

The sounds of the caravan got louder, and then new voices and accents were added to the mix. When Joseph looked up, he saw a circle of strange faces looking down at him from the top of the cistern.

My brothers really and truly are trying to sell me as a slave to these foreigners. That's insane! That's detestable! That's . . . That's . . . That's . . . probably better than the other option I heard them discussing. It's obvious they won't let me go free for fear of what I'll tell Dad. Being a slave will at least keep me alive with a chance for escaping at some point. Then I can plot my revenge for what they've done to me.

"God, help me and please stay with me," Joseph prayed as he saw Judah being lowered into the pit on a rope. Judah wrapped both the end of the rope and his own arms around Joseph, signaled to their brothers, and both men were lifted out of the pit.

"Well, here he is," Levi said to the Ishmaelites. "As you can see, he's a strong and healthy lad of seventeen years. He can work all day."

The Ishmaelites examined Joseph from head to toe, checked his teeth, and felt of his muscles. Then they huddled and discussed him in a language Joseph couldn't understand. Finally one of them turned to the brothers and said, "We'll give you ten pieces of silver for him."

"Ten?" gasped Judah. "He's worth at least fifty. You're not going to find a better or more intelligent slave anywhere for that price."

"Don't try that line on us," said one of the traders. "You boys are desperate to get rid of him. We'll take him off your hands and pay you fifteen pieces of silver. You're in no position to bargain."

Judah looked at his brothers and mouthed a number. When they nodded, he turned and said, "Thirty."

"Twenty—and that's our last offer. Take it or we leave him with you."

Joseph's brothers looked at each other, nodded, and took the offer. The Ishmaelites counted out twenty shekels of silver, put a rope around Joseph's wrists, attached the other end of the rope to a wagon, and led him away.

If you enjoyed
Saul's Quest, **read on for a preview of**

Wizard's Gambit

**A science fiction / fantasy novel
by Bill Kincaid**

Jackzen awakened from a sound sleep when his wife clutched his arm and fearfully asked, "What was that?"

"What's what?" His voice was groggy, but his muscles tensed.

They both listened intently for a moment, clutching each other in the predawn darkness.

"That!" Annika responded as a crash from the front room was quickly followed by the sound of loud footsteps rushing toward their bedroom, accompanied by the light of four burning torches.

Jackzen tossed aside the covers and started to spring from the bed, but was immediately forced back by a spear that cut him in his chest. He dropped onto the bed, clutching the top bedspread to his chest to stanch the bleeding. Only then did he look at the men surrounding him.

Soldiers. Or enforcers. Armed, surly, and mean.

"What's the meaning of this outrage?" he demanded.

"We're here to collect what you owe the Crown," responded one of them, a tall burly man standing to the right of the one who held the spear that had wounded him.

"We've already paid everything we owe the king," Jackzen protested. "All taxes and fees that were due, plus the extra assessments that enforcers demanded."

"That's what you claim," the enforcer who was apparently in charge replied. "We say you haven't paid what you owe."

"Kratzl!" Jackzen swore. "I can prove I paid it."

"Let's see your proof."

"Let me get up, and I'll get my receipt."

The officer motioned for his men to allow Jackzen to rise from the bed. Still holding the bedspread against his chest, Jackzen made his way to his dresser, rummaged through a drawer, and withdrew the vital document. He handed it to the officer triumphantly.

The officer read it carefully by the light of one of the torches, and then burned it in the fire.

"What other proof do you have to offer?"

"Hey!" Jackzen objected. "You can't do that!"

"I just did. What other proof do you have?"

"I shouldn't need any other proof. That receipt showed I paid all charges in full."

"Receipt? I don't see any receipt." The officer turned to his men. "Do any of you see a receipt?"

They laughed, sneered, and shook their heads.

"What proof do you now have to offer?"

Jackzen sputtered but held his tongue. "What is it you want?" he asked.

"I want your teenage daughter."

"Marza? Why?"

"Come off it, Jackzen. You're smarter than that. You know why."

"No! You have no right!" Jackzen yelled while lunging at the officer before being clubbed over the head by another enforcer.

"We have all the rights," Jackzen heard as he slipped from consciousness. "We're the king's enforcers."

About the Author

Although Bill Kincaid spent over 35 years practicing law in Texas, he started out as a writer and journalist. He was sports editor and political editor for his high school paper, edited his university newspaper, and worked for several Texas newspapers before earning his doctor of jurisprudence degree from Texas Tech University's School of Law. Several of his articles and columns received state-wide honors.

Now that Kincaid is slowing down his legal practice, he finally has time to return to his writing roots, publishing two books in 2013 that are almost as different from each other as day is from night.

Nicodemus' Quest is a Christian historical fiction novel that makes as much use of Kincaid's ability to do detailed research as it does of his ability to tell a good story. *The Baptist Standard* called the book "a compelling, inventive, moving novel . . . a great story" and said that "extensive biblical, historical, geographical, archeological, and linguistic research exudes from each page."

On the other hand, *Ronald Raygun and the Sweeping Beauty* is a fractured fairy tale that satirizes such well known stories as *Sleeping Beauty, The Princess and the Pea,* and *Cinderella.* What makes the story even more fun is the humor that is woven throughout, not to mention various political references that permeate the work. Some are obvious (such as in the title), but most are extremely subtle and unobtrusive.

Kincaid is continuing to write on varied topics. In 2014, he published *Saul's Quest*, a novel about the Apostle Paul's life through his first missionary journey. *Wizard's Gambit*, his first science fiction fantasy, is the first book in the Ventryvian Legacy Series. He is also conducting research for a second book about Paul's life that will continue the story told in *Saul's Quest*.

He and his wife, Audette, have been married for more than 45 years and have three adult children, Cheryl-Annette, Christina, and Sharlene.

Made in the USA
Middletown, DE
28 July 2024